WHISPERS OF A KILLER

WHISPS BOOK ONE

JEN HAEGER

SCARSDALE PUBLISHING

This is a work of fiction. Names, characters, places, and incidents are either the product of the author's imagination or are used fictitiously, and any resemblance to actual persons living or dead, business establishments, events, or locales, is entirely coincidental.

ISBN 13: 9781953100016

Cover design by dreams2media

First Trade Paperback Printing by Broken Arm Publishing: June 2019

10 9 8 7 6 5 4 3 2

MTV

CNBC

Harvard

Los Angeles Police Department

The Vatican

Skype

New York Times

ComGlobal

Botox

FutureCon

Ford Focus

Fox Local News at 7 Las Vegas

Excedrin

San Francisco Tribune

Mashable.com

Fat Tire beer

The Bachelorette

Gatorade

Kickstarter

Tylenol

HBO

The Daily Show

Comedy Central

Chevy Impala

NASCAR

Bolero (song)

Tyvek

Styrofoam

Bellevue Hospital

Chicago Tribune

Kwik Lube

Kirby

CHAPTER 1

"What is a WHISP? Nothing...if not a reflection of ourselves as a society."

Sharon Vale, Philosopher of Technology, Santa Clara University

THE COURTROOM IS SILENT AS THE JURY FILES IN, save for the muffled grief of the victims' family members. I'm surprised by the amount of time it's taken them to reach a verdict, but as they shuffle by Chester, none of them look at her. Not once in all my decades in court have I ever seen a jury avoid eye contact with a defendant they've found not guilty. The muscles in my jaw and the back of my neck relax, but then I tense again. I remind myself this is no ordinary case, and the jury may have another reason for shunning Chester, the same reason, in fact, I'm averting my gaze from her.

Rachel Iris Chester is sprawled in her chair doodling on a legal pad with a felt-tipped pen. From the sallow and disgusted expression of her court-appointed counsel, I'm guessing her drawings are fairly grotesque, though I'm not at a good angle to see them. Not that I'd want to or need to, since as head investigator on her case, I've already poured over notebooks filled with her violent and disturbing renderings. Chester's hair falls in oily brown curtains to the shoulders of her orange jump suit, and on her face she wears a sneer of indifference to the goings on around her. But it's not her posture or sketches or attitude that disturbs me, it's her WHISP.

About a foot behind Chester, right in front of the wooden rail separating the spectators in the courtroom from the active participants, is a fuzzy grey shadow. It sits in midair mimicking Chester, leaning back, legs splayed with one hand holding a phantom pad and the other moving over it making ghost drawings of invisible ink. I don't want to look at the thing, but I'm drawn to it. Shivering, I will myself to look away and find the gaunt, haunted faces of Mr. and Mrs. Rose and their daughter Paris. The Roses, Simon and Ann, faces taut with grief and anticipation, are watching the jury. Paris is staring daggers at Chester's back, or rather through her WHISP to her back, as she's been doing the entire trial. Their son Michael was likely Chester's first victim, though we couldn't find any definitive evidence linking her to his murder, except the horribly unique modus operandi of the killing.

Next to the Roses, Ms. Beene sobs quietly into her handkerchief. On her left, her daughter-in-law Lucy holds her hand in a tight grip of commiseration though her eyes are clear and dry. Lucy's husband, Jacob Beene, was Chester's third victim, and I'm confident that a shoe impression and trace evidence collected at the coffee shop he worked at will secure a guilty verdict. My gaze wanders from Lucy Beene to the Hunts. Henry Hunt, their only son, was Chester's last victim, and his case is the strongest we have against Chester. In addition to trace and blood evidence linking her to his apartment, she had kept a tuft of his hair.

Behind the Hunts, an assembly of Infantes mourn son, father, brother, cousin, and uncle Diego, though his murder was not brought to trial today. Not enough evidence, yet so many grieving faces. The courtroom is filled with friends and family of Chester's six victims, all waiting for justice to be served. The only notable absence is the niece of the second-to-last victim, Grant Wilcox. I had spoken to the woman on several occasions about her uncle and the circumstances of his death. It was her opinion the man deserved to die, so I'm not surprised she didn't fly in from Phoenix to attend the trial.

As always, I feel connected to the families, yet I'm separate. Having testified earlier today, I'm with the other witnesses in the section on the judge's right. Also, I've been given a chance to speak, unlike the family members.

"Foreperson, has the jury reached a verdict?"

My focus is drawn back to the front of the court by the judge's words.

The foreperson, a solid African American woman in her fifties with tightly curled, greying hair, wearing a turquoise blouse and skirt, nods with a professional air. "We have, Your Honor."

She hands the court clerk a folded slip of paper. The clerk in turn hands the verdict to the judge, who unfolds it and scans the contents, his face a mask of impassivity.

"Will the defendant please rise?"

Chester's lawyer has to nudge her with an elbow and whisper in her ear to get Chester to comply. The quiet of the courtroom is shattered when Chester pushes her chair backward with an ear-assailing screech and then stands. The fluid movements of her WHISP incites a renewed chill down my spine, which I try to ignore. It's almost over now.

"What is your verdict?"

Now many of the jurors turn to stare at Chester, including the forewoman whose objectivity is now belied with a frown.

"We, the jury, find the defendant, Rachel Chester, in the charge of murder in the first degree of Grant Wilcox, not guilty."

Fuck. The evidence in Wilcox's murder hadn't been as strong as for Hunt's, but I still thought the jury would understand it's a lot easier to get blood spatter on your shirt while you're murdering someone rather than during some bullshit imaginary fist fight with them. Razors of anger dissolve into a cold and empty hole in my stomach even as it clenches, because I know what's coming. If the jury didn't find Chester guilty of killing Wilcox, then...

"In the charge of murder in the first degree of Jacob Beene, we find the defendant, Rachel Chester, not guilty."

Ms. Beene's wail echoes through the room and I can't look at her. *I promised her justice for her son, goddammit!*

"In the charge of murder in the first degree of Henry Hunt"—*Oh god, please. Please*—"we the jury find the defendant, Rachel Iris Chester, guilty."

Thank you. I think I hear Paris Rose telling Chester to "Burn in hell," but it's difficult to hear over Ms. Beene's anguish. Relief washes through me, but the sweetness of the victory, of putting a killer behind bars, is tainted for me. Twice I had failed to produce enough evidence to convince the jury of Chester's guilt. I'm still reeling from the idea that Chester came within one clump of hair of walking out of the courtroom a free woman, when the judge announces the date of the sentencing hearing. I pray it will be life in prison without the possibility of parole. It's the strictest punishment New York has to offer and, for the briefest instant, I wish I lived in Texas. Then the gavel hits the block with a resounding crack and the whole court is on its feet. It's all over. The case, the trial, and my life as a cop.

CHAPTER 2

"We provide a service and do not, nor have we ever,
made claims as to the inherent safety of using that
service. If an individual wants to partake of our service,
they do so, and have always done so, at their own risk."

*Albin Corvet, CEO, WorldComVerse, excerpt from The People
vs. WorldComVerse*

*Six years old, I'm in the hallway rubbing my eyes. Something has
woken me and I've stumbled out of my bedroom to find out what it was.
There's a glowing light at the end of the hall and as I get closer, I see the
television in the living room is on and black and white static flickers
across the screen. I'm wondering why someone left the TV on when
suddenly a shadow steps in front of the television. Backlit by the static,
all I see is an inky outline of a person, but it doesn't match the shape of
my mother, my father, or my big brother. I gasp, and the outline turns its
featureless, black face toward me. I scream.*

I jolt awake. Heart racing, it takes me a minute to recognize
the ceiling fan, the comfortable sagging of the mattress, and
Ben's soft snoring. It was the nightmare again. I'm in the apartment, I'm an adult, and I'm safe. My taut muscles ease into

relaxation. Exhausted, I know there will be no more sleep tonight. There never is after the nightmare. Carefully, I extract myself from the bed, trying not to disturb Ben or Grumps, our furry Persian baby, and exit the bedroom. Out in the hallway, my heartrate jumps again briefly, but then I'm in the bathroom with the door shut and the light on. I turn on the hot water tap of the sink and lean against the counter. Meeting the eyes of my reflection, I sigh. "Time for therapy again?"

———

BEN ENTERS THE KITCHEN, HIS LOOSELY TIED ROBE just barely concealing his muscled chest. "Morning, love." He smiles.

I'm in the living room, ostensibly sorting important papers and weeding out those not worthy of making the move, but actually, I've been staring at the same page for a few minutes now. I force my face into a cheerful expression. "Morning."

Ben isn't fooled. He revs up the Keurig and frowns. "How long have you been up?"

"A little while."

"Uh huh. More nightmares?"

I place the paper I've been holding in the keep pile, though I've already forgotten what it was. "Just the one."

"Do you think you should call Dr. Fritz?"

Ben suggesting it makes me cranky. "I'm fine. Or rather, I'll be fine once we get outta here. We've got way too much to do still, and he probably won't have any appointments available until after we move anyway."

Collecting his coffee mug, Ben joins me in the living room. "I'm sure he'd be able to fit you in."

I mutter something that could be construed as a maybe and turn my attention back to the stacks of papers on the coffee table. Ben sits next to me on the couch and runs the fingers of his free hand through my hair. "Babe, I'm worried about you. You have to start getting some sleep."

He's wrong, though he means well. Sleep isn't exactly the problem. I rarely have trouble falling asleep. But I'd kill to get some decent rest.

———

BAGELS, CREAM CHEESE, AND SEVERAL CUPS OF warm, caffeinated beverages later, we're both loading cardboard boxes with books and light, bulky things like Tupperware so that we can actually lift the boxes. Ben has the same look on his face he's had since my retirement. The gentle lines around his mouth and eyes are trying to be happy. Happy I'm retired, happy we're both getting away from disturbed criminals and destroyed lives; the lie he's not only been telling me for almost a month, but himself. I tape up a box wondering if he knows I know he's unhappy. He doesn't want to leave the city, doesn't want to be seven states away from Lincoln, but we have a plan and he made a promise. The thought of being so far away from my only child breaks my heart, but Lincoln is even more stubborn than I am, and he won't leave New York, at least, not now.

So, we pack in a silence heavy with things we want to say, my eyes still red and grainy with exhaustion. It's almost a palpable relief when the phone rings. Ben is closer and faster and I'm removing Grumps from a half-filled box, so Ben answers it.

"'Lo." The congenial expression on his face fades quickly as he turns to me. "Yes, she is. May I ask who's calling?"

A scowl has taken up residence on Ben's lips. I set Grumps down on the couch.

"Uh huh. Just a minute." Ben places a hand over the receiver and sighs.

"Who is it?"

"Says his name's Crone. Lieutenant Crone, NYPD."

The name doesn't ring any immediate bells, but there'd been a lot of changes in my precinct in just the short time since I'd left the force. I reach for the phone. Ben hands it to me stiffly.

"Hello?"

"Lieutenant Harbinger?" The voice is gruff with a hint of irritation.

The lieutenant part isn't quite true anymore, but I much prefer it to Mrs. "Yes."

"My name's Lieutenant Crone."

"What can I do for you, Lieutenant?"

"I need you to come down to the precinct ASAP."

He says the acronym like a word, military style. I've been trying to keep my face neutral for Ben's sake, but this shatters my façade of nonchalance, so I turn away and drift into the kitchen. Bracing the phone between my ear and shoulder, I cinch my robe tighter around me. "What's this all about?"

"It's about Rachel Chester, Lieutenant."

CHAPTER 3

"The question isn't whether an individual with a WHISP is a fit parent, but rather the question is whether a child should be forced to be exposed to the same environment which created the parent's WHISP."

Wendy Bleeker, Esq., California Department of Public Health, Child Safety Division

ALL THE AIR FLIES OUT OF MY LUNGS AT ONCE, AND the kitchen wobbles unsteadily in my vision. This isn't happening. It isn't real. I can't tell if I'm awake or in a new nightmare. Chester is in jail, tried, convicted, and sentenced. Anyone calling me with her name in their mouths who isn't a reporter has bad news.

"Lieutenant?"

Crone's voice solidifies the world, and I take in a deep breath. "Tell me."

"I'd rather you just came down to the precinct." Resistance.

I'm not having it. "Lieutenant, Rachel Chester has threatened my life and the lives of my family members multiple times. If there's some technicality or an appeal or she's escaped from prison, I have a right to know. Now."

"Nothing like that. There's been a murder."

"If Chester is still in jail, I don't see what that has to do with her, or me. I'm not sure if they told you, Lieutenant Crone, but I'm retired."

"I wish you would just come down—"

"And I wish that you would stop bullshitting and tell me what's going on." I spin and spot Ben hovering in the kitchen doorway. I can't blame him for eavesdropping. It isn't as if he couldn't hear every word from the living room.

"Copycat. A good one, too. Chief said we'd better consult with you, you being the expert on Chester and all."

I can't meet Ben's eyes. "Yeah. I guess I am." This is total crap and I should just tell Crone no, but he mentioned the Chief asking for me. Chief Lowman wouldn't have allowed some schmuck lieutenant to call me if it wasn't important. Turning, I feel Ben's stare of daggers piercing my back. "Okay. I'll be there in an hour."

"Until then."

Placing the phone in its charger, I turn to face Ben.

"Be where in an hour?"

"The precinct."

Ben stares me down.

"There's… They want me to consult on a case."

"Did you happen to mention to them that you're retired?"

"It's one of my old cases. They just want my opinion on… new evidence." I brush past him into the hall, but he grabs my arm.

"Which case?"

I swallow hard. I've already skirted the truth enough to have gotten his dander up. "Rachel Chester."

Ben's grip on my arm slackens. "Mother fucker."

I move past him and head to the bedroom. "No, that was a different case."

"That's not funny."

I want to tell him it would've had the whole homicide department rolling, but he never understood the desperate need for dark humor when dealing with the worst of humanity and the horrors that follow in their wake. "Sorry."

As I'm pulling black slacks, a white blouse, and a black blazer I never thought I'd have to wear again from the closet, Ben appears in the bedroom doorway. "She's not going to get off, is she? You said there's new evidence?"

"Chester's going to rot in jail for the rest of her life. This is just... I'll be home in a few hours." I head for the bathroom, but Ben blocks the door.

"Sylvia—"

"Look, Ben, I can't just turn off being a cop. I can't just say screw you to all of those victims' families and tell them I'm sorry, but I'm too busy packing to tie up any loose ends with my old cases. You know I have to go."

His eyes go soft. "But it's Chester."

I move him out of my way with a gentle hand on his shoulder. "I know."

———

BEN SAYS LITTLE MORE UNTIL HE'S KISSING ME goodbye at the door. "Text me when you're heading home."

"I will."

Then I'm driving to the precinct, focusing on the road in front of me as best I can while, in my mind, the gruesome crime scenes of Chester's case play back on fast forward. If this is a copycat killer, it will be my first, but it isn't terribly surprising. The case made national news not only because of the brutal nature of the crimes or the fact she was a female serial killer, but because Chester has a WHISP. The overcharged media exploded when she was arrested. While the pro-WHISP lobby debated the ethics of punishing a WHISP for its human's crimes, the anti-WHISP lobby used the case as proof of the inherent evil of WHISPs. You had to be living under a rock or in a tech-free cabin in the wilds of Montana not to have heard about Rachel Chester.

So, in retrospect, a copycat seemed inevitable. But why the hell did NYPD need my input to deal with one? I'd kept painstaking notes on Chester throughout the investigation. Those notes should've contained more than enough details to deal with a copycat. There had to be more to the story, but as I fought through traffic, I couldn't figure out what. Whoever this Chester-wannabe was, I damned him or her for not waiting just another couple of months to start their killing spree. By then Ben and I would have been on the road with no turning back, not ten minutes away where some jackass detective on a power trip felt like he could order me to come down to my old precinct. I pull into a visitor spot, turn off the car and stare up at the rearview mirror. "Yeah, but you're the idiot who can't let it go."

Sighing, I get out of the car and stride up to the front door. A young, blond officer exiting the precinct holds the door for me before a spark of recognition fires in his eyes and a wide smile spreads across his face like a sunrise. "Lieutenant Harbinger! Nice to see you, Ma'am. I take it you haven't headed west yet?"

"Not quite yet, Schmitty. How's the works?"

"Can't complain. But what brings you down here? Forget your favorite stapler?"

I smile. "Give you three guesses and the first two don't count."

His blue eyes narrow and his smile sags. "It's that 187

they're all talking about, yeah? They get you to come back to work?"

"Naw, just consulting."

"Heh, like Sherlock Holmes."

"Exactly, except for the cocaine. Now Schmitty, you won't tell anyone I've been by, right? Wouldn't want folks to get jealous that I didn't visit."

"You can count on me, Lieutenant. You take care and have a good trip if I don't see ya again before you leave."

"I will."

I watch Schmitty skip down the last few steps and I wave to him when he reaches the bottom. He's a good kid, and I'm glad I won't be here when he takes a bullet or a bribe or when the stress of the job breaks his spirit. As the familiar scents of the precinct fill my nostrils, mostly stale coffee and pungent floor cleaner, I feel a bittersweet comfort, but it's my home away from home no more. Resisting the urge to walk right to the back, I glide up to the front desk and an unfamiliar redhead looks up from her computer. "Can I help you?"

"I'm Sylvia Harbinger. I'm here to see Lieutenant Crone. He's expecting me."

She picks up the phone, consults a phone list, and taps three digits. During the pause that follows, she gives me a perfunctory smile. "A Ms. Harbringer here to see Lieutenant Crone."

Not very observant, this one. I want to tap my wedding ring and correct her pronunciation, but I restrain myself. My being edgy has nothing to do with her and I don't want to take out crap on the poor girl.

"Uh huh. Thanks." She hangs up the phone. "Lieutenant Crone said to go right back to the briefing room. Said you'd know the way?"

"I do, thank you."

Here we go again.

CHAPTER 4

"Many have blamed the Department of Energy for their lack of regulations with regards to magnetic fields, but the truth is, technology is neither a fad nor something that Americans are willing to live without. I think if you asked most people whether they'd give up their computers and cell phones in order to avoid developing a WHISP, they would think you were insane."

Eric Dugan, Journalist for Technology Magazine

LIEUTENANT CRONE IS A LOT LIKE I PICTURED HIM: A big pain-in-the-ass in a discount suit. His stubble is impressive, as are his bright white teeth and the mustard stain on his already hideous tie. His hand is a big hunk of clammy meat swallowing my relatively normal sized one and crushing it for good measure. Years of dealing with inflated male egos exactly like his keep me from wincing during the introductions.

"Lieutenant Harbinger, it's a pleasure to finally meet you."

"Lieutenant Crone."

"Please sit down."

I park in one of the comfortable black rollers at the large

oval conference desk but keep a straight back. It's just the two of us and the room feels too big. "Where's the chief?"

"Trying to put a cap on the press."

"Ah, right. Okay. Hit me. Why did I need to come all the way down here?"

Crone smirks. "They told me you were the no-nonsense type." He flips open a folder and drops it in front of me before plunking down in the seat next to mine. "This happened three days ago in SoHo. Her name was Alice. Alice Petrie."

A woman? I'm struggling to think about what a woman's murder has to do with Chester's six-man killing spree when glossy photos of a familiar scene assault my eyes. Even knowing what I was probably going to see doesn't change the awfulness of it. I examine each photo in turn, suppressing emotion. It's all so similar to Chester's MO, but the fact that it's a female victim is throwing me.

"I'm sure that you can see why we called you 'all the way down here.' This is too carbon copy. Either someone on the force made a pretty penny selling your crime scene notes or Chester had an accomplice who's taken it upon himself to continue that psycho's good work."

I don't look up from the pictures or correct Crone's misassumption or misuse of pronouns. If Chester had an accomplice, it wouldn't have been a man. "There was never any evidence of an accomplice."

"So your file says. But then, how do you explain that?" Crone points a bulky finger at the photo in my hand. It's a close-up of a cell phone lodged in a woman's throat. A detail of the original murders held very quiet and need-to-know.

"Chester could have said something to someone, written a letter; hell, she could've tweeted it."

"Survey says no, and I know you see more little odds and ends that no one's supposed to know about."

I set down the photo and rub my temples. "That still

doesn't mean there's an accomplice. I know that this may come as a shock to you, Crone, but there are such things as dirty cops. It's like you said before, probably an inside leak." Even as I speak, I'm wracking my brain trying to remember what details I'd actually put in my reports and which were in my personal notes that no one but me had access to.

"Chief thinks there's enough doubt, and this case is sufficiently ugly that he wants this thing put to bed quickly and quietly. He wants you to come back. Help solve this thing before it's one big shitstorm again."

"And just why does he think I'd do that?"

"Said he'd consider it a personal favor, and also that Sylvia Harbinger didn't leave shit just hanging."

What Crone doesn't say is that no one knows Chester like I do, and with the threat of another serial, the chief probably had no choice in calling me back in. I snort. "Bastard. Don't suppose I can get copies of all this to compare with my personal notes."

"But of course, Lieutenant."

I gather up the photos in the file and pass it over to Crone.

"Does this mean you're putting yourself on the case?"

"It *means* that I need to compare stuff with my personal notes."

"Uh huh." Crone takes the file and walks out leaving me alone in the briefing room.

It might be the first time I've ever really been alone in here. Sitting back in the chair, I close my eyes, but the images from the photos are still there as if they've been photocopied onto the backs of my eyelids. I don't try to kid myself that there's going to be a fast arrest here. If Crone and company had any leads at all, I wouldn't be here. There's also no sense telling myself I can just let this go and have someone else deal with it. That isn't going to happen. Now I just have to find a way of doing it without wrecking my marriage. I can hear Ben's every argument already in my ears: "They can't ask you to do this, you're retired. You promised, Sylvy. How can you even think about doing this after all that this case put you through the first time?"

His yet-to-be-spoken points aren't invalid, and how am I going to go through this all again? This case, my last case, sent me into therapy and came damn close to ending my marriage. Only my agreeing to early retirement and Ben agreeing to move out of the city kept us together. *What was the saying about compromise? A conclusion where both participants walk away unhappy?* But seriously, I have to figure out how I'm going to convince Ben that finishing this case, really finishing this case, is the only option for me. *Dammit.*

I am hating Chester all over again. Hating a world where someone like her is even allowed to exist. But also hating myself for allowing her to get to me. "You're tougher than this, Sylvia, ol' girl. You'll take down this worthless excuse for a human, just like you took down the original. Then it's a cozy cabin and serene mountains and a proper retirement."

"Gosh, I miss these little conversations we used to have without me."

Maybe if I'd gotten a decent night sleep, I'd have bolted out of my chair at the chief sneaking up on me whilst I was talking to myself, but today I can't manage it. I do spin the chair to face him and stand up. "Chief. Are we fighting the good fight today?"

His mocha lips thin. "You mean the one against the press? I suppose."

"I mean the one against monsters like Chester."

"We could be."

CHAPTER 5

"The WHISP phenomenon is real. But it is not a reason to fear. It is not a reason to panic. Nor is it the next stage in human evolution. WHISPs are merely a byproduct of technology. Soon we will discover under what circumstances they are produced, and how to prevent and eventually eradicate them. This is a global occurrence, but should in no way be construed as a global crisis."

President Hannah Truefall, excerpt Presidential Address, May 2ⁿᵈ, 2030

CHIEF LOWMAN ISN'T MY POP AND HE DIDN'T SAY he'd be disappointed in me if I didn't come back on board until this copycat was put away, but he's still a father-figure to me, despite my age, and I know he would be. But it isn't a reason Ben will understand. I'm not sure there is a reason he will understand, but I have to try. He's still in the living room packing when I get back from the precinct, a folder of photo-copied pages from the copycat murder under my arm.

Hearing me come in, he meets me in the hallway to give my lips a peck. "So, how'd it go?"

"Not great. Let's, ah, sit down, okay?"

Ben eyes the folder under my arm. "What's that?"

"Case file."

"On Chester?"

"Not exactly." I brush past Ben and head to the living room. I weave around boxes, sit on the couch and set the file on the coffee table.

Ben follows, but his face is already a blank mask behind which anger bubbles. He doesn't sit with me on the couch but chooses an armchair instead. "Tell me."

I do. I tell him everything that Crone told me, everything the chief said, and everything I could glean from the file in the short time I'd studied it. Ben sits in silence, his expression unchanged and his posture rigid. He doesn't nod or give any indication that he's listening at all save his brown eyes locked on me in steady regard. I finish. The silence stretches. I try to stay still and neutral. If I don't give Ben a chance to give me his opinion first, without resistance, then he may bottle it up and never tell me what he truly thinks. I must be patient.

Finally, after swallowing several times, he says, "You didn't tell them 'no,' did you?"

I choose my words carefully, "I didn't tell them 'yes,' either."

"So, what did you say?"

"I told them that I'd have to consider, but that I *would* compare this case with my personal notes to see if anything sticks out."

Ben stands and turns to the window. "I know that look. You already think there's a connection. That you might've missed something."

"Rachel Chester is a loner, and there was never any evidence of an accomplice...but there are similarities, details that Chester or someone else in the know must have shared with someone."

Ben doesn't look at me. "You already know I don't think you should do this, and I don't want you to, so I don't feel like this is much of a discussion. We almost didn't make it through this case once already, and to be honest with you, I don't think we're out of the woods yet. And now you're asking me to let you get dragged back into it. What do you want me to say?"

He isn't wrong. Not in one thing he's saying. In this moment, I might be choosing between saving my marriage and catching a killer. I love Ben, so much it hurts sometimes, and there could be no one else in the world willing to put up with my own special brand of bullshit, but people had died, and more people were going to die, and if I'd missed something in the initial investigation, then their deaths would all be on me. *Could I live with a failed marriage? With Ben as just a friend, splitting holidays with Lincoln?* My heart feels crushed even thinking about it, but maybe. What I couldn't live with was willfully letting a mistake of mine get people killed. I only hope Ben will understand. I stand and join him at the window without touching him.

"You're right. This isn't much of a discussion, and I'm sorry for that. I will understand if…if you can't do this with me. But, Ben, if I missed something, if I screwed up this case somehow, people have died because of it, and more people are going to die because of it. Because of my fuck up."

He turns to me, eyes blazing. "You don't know that. Sylvy, they can catch this bastard without you."

"Maybe. But what if they don't? How many lives is that chance worth? One? Two?"

His gaze returns to the cityscape outside the window. "You realize the position I'm in, right? I let you do this and go through hell again or I say no and I'm the asshole for leaving you at a time like this. You might forgive me, but what about Lincoln?"

"Don't do that. Lincoln's a grown man now. He's got your

brains and my moxie. He'd understand." I swallow and take his hand. "I know I'm asking for a lot. And I know I don't really deserve this from you. But I'd also like to think that because of the shit we've gone through in the past, we're going to be able to handle this shit better. We already know what to expect, at least the general flavor of shit if not the specific dish."

Ben cracks a smile but quashes it quickly. His hand returns my grip as he looks into my eyes. "One month. I know you have to fix this, but, at some point, you also have to let it go."

I can't suppress the flare of anger that goes off in me. It's just so Ben to think the case could be resolved so quickly and easily, but then I pause and ask myself what exactly I was hoping for. *What did I think he was going to say?* "Sure, sweetie pie, take all the time you need." *Yeah right.* And I think I can vaguely see his point through the haze of my emotions. Eventually, maybe I will have to let it go. Maybe not in one month, but someday.

"A month."

We seal Ben's ultimatum with a kiss.

CHAPTER 6

Population of the United States with WHISP: 16.5
million or approximately 5%

U.S. Census Bureau 2027

THREE DAYS LATER, CRONE AND I ARE MAKING OUR
way into the depths of Rikers. There's an aura of palpable
hatred coming from the place that's hard to ignore as we pass
block after block. A few new, colorful sexual insults are thrown
my way, but they bounce off the armor I've already erected for
Chester. I will my face blank, my hands steady, and my pace
unbroken. Crone is smirking like he's enjoying the atmosphere,
and he may very well be. Some cops get off on seeing perps
behind bars, like it's a validation of their work. Not me. I'm not
naïve enough to think prisons are or do any good. More criminal shit goes down in Rikers on a typical Friday night than in
an entire week in the scummiest parts of the city. Prisons are a
necessary evil, with evil being the key word.

It does give me the smallest relief to know that some individuals are behind these bars though, and right now Rachel
Chester is at the top of the list. The journey to get to Chester is

longer than most. Because of the high profile nature of her case, she's kept in special solitary and she's not supposed to have any visitors. Of course, they make an exception for detectives, especially when the case goes from solved to ongoing. Chester's lawyer is no doubt wetting himself at the possibility we may have screwed something up, but the chief's already told him not to get too excited. We're playing things off like we're dealing with a typical copycat, not a possible accomplice or someone Chester may have personally coached. That's a sobering thought: personal murder coaching.

The arrangements for the interview are awkward. Chester is shackled to a chair in her cell with the solid metal door open, and there are two chairs for Crone and me to sit in just outside. The guard who's been leading us opens the barred door leading into Chester's private, dead end hallway and gestures us through but doesn't follow.

"You've done this before?"

I hold up the panic button device issued at entry. "She twitches, I press this, you bust in, guns blazing."

The guard's face is stony. "When you're done, approach this door but stay behind the line. I'll close the inmate's door before I open this one."

He presses a button on the wall and the door slides shut between us with a clang that I feel in my bones. The churning in my stomach has reached a nauseating pitch, but I can't let anything show. I can't give Chester anything. Crone's presence should be reassuring, but somehow it's only making things worse. My not coming alone will seem like weakness to Chester. Maybe it is. I didn't fight Crone on his being here, even though I don't think Chester will give us anything with him present. I tell myself it's all fine. When Chester gives us nothing, I'll have ammunition against Crone being here next time.

We reach the chairs and sit. I avoid looking at Chester until

I absolutely have to. When I do, she's leering at me from her chair, her eyes full of quiet malice. I can't believe she wasn't always like this, that she once was a student in the same program at NYU as my son, worked in the same lab. My fingers are numb on the arms of my chair. At first, I don't see her WHISP in the shadowy depths of the cell, but then my pupils adjust and its shape emerges from the darkness. It's an inky mirror of Chester, also leering at me, but without eyes.

"I knew it was you." Chester's voice is a flat Midwest drawl, nasally and ugly. She completely ignores Crone. I knew she would.

Crone dislikes being ignored. "Didn't know she was a fucking psychic. I suppose you know why we're here too, then."

"To what do I owe this honor Detective Harbinger? Still looking for a confession? Hardly seems necessary now. Or did you just miss me and Ray?"

Hiding a shudder by scratching my neck, I finally speak to her. "You're a smart gal, Chester. I'm pretty sure you know why we're here."

The wheels are turning behind her eyes, always calculating. If you could catch Chester's interest, it was unwavering. I caught her interest, Crone didn't, simple as that. Some people were inconsequential to Chester, while others were games to her, puzzles to be systematically explored, dominated, broken down, and dismantled.

"You sound so bold, Detective. The therapy must be going well then."

In my periphery, I spot a small smirk on Crone's face. Asshole. He doesn't constitute enough of a person to need therapy.

"Well, if this isn't a social visit, I certainly hope you didn't bring this ape along for a conjugal visit…"

The ape comment's enough for Crone. "Come on, Chester, nothing you want to tell us about? Don't even wanna gloat?"

A slight twitch of my finger is all that betrays my desire to reach out and slap Crone across his big stupid mouth. I have no idea where he picked up his interrogation skills, or poker skills, but he's just shown our whole hand.

Chester shifts in her chair and her WHISP shifts too, reminding me of its presence with a jolt. Her face lights up like Orphan Annie's on her first Christmas with Daddy Warbucks. Chester now knows what we know without us being able to know if she'd known before.

"Gloat? Why whatever would I have to glo—oh, ooooh! Something's happened hasn't it? Something you think I'd be *proud* of. Now let me see, what could it be, what could it be?"

A cracking sound comes from Crone's jaw.

Interjecting before Crone can say anything else catastrophically moronic, "Actually, I didn't think you'd be proud of it, at all. If fact, I thought you'd be kinda pissed off. Thought you were more of a one woman show, myself."

"Oh, but I am, Detective. You know that." Chester writhes in her chair, causing her WHISP to undulate behind her.

"Do I?"

Chester grins, showing straight, white teeth. "You should."

I just stare into those cold eyes and wait. Chester likes to talk, and I wanted her to monologue, maybe give something away in her smugness. There's something else too. For the briefest moment I see something behind her icy stare, a flicker of something, a crack, but before I can analyze it, of course, Crone is feeling left out and it hurts his delicate, fucking, baby feelings.

"I don't know you, chicky, why don't you enlighten me?"

And it's over. Chester's face turns like my college boyfriend's face turned when we were in the preludes of sex and my grandmother called. The mood is spoiled. Chester won't be giving us anything on the copycat, at least not today. Ignoring Crone, she says, "Detective, I assume you are responsible for keeping the monkey on its leash and cleaning up its doo-doo, so I think it's time for his walkies. Don't you?"

I do, in fact, but fuck if I'm going to agree with her...but then an angle presents itself. It's a shitty angle, one that I feel grimy pursuing, but my delicate baby feelings are less important than stopping people from being brutally murdered, so I go with it. "Yeah, you'll have to excuse detective Crone, he didn't get his nap today. But why don't you and I just pretend he's not here?"

She considers my words, or at least pretends to consider them. I'm pretty sure she sees through my flimsy "us against him" ruse, but there's always the possibility she'll go with it just to fuck with me, to try to get back inside my head. Crone's shockingly silent. I'd like to think he's finally wised up to him not helping matters, but more likely he's just reeling from me insulting him. I don't even flick my eyes to him to see which it is because my eyes are still locked on Chester's, and they're starting to burn. *Can't blink. Can't blink.* Her irises shift subtly.

"Tempting, Detective, very tempting, but I think no. Come back without your pet sometime, but today's interview is over."

CHAPTER 7

"In what way has your WHISP affected your acting career?"

"Oh, I think that it's opened up a lot of WHISP-specific roles for me."

"What about non-WHISP roles, are you still getting those?"

"Sure. With digital technology, they can pretty much, like, photo-shop my WHISP out of any shot."

"Have you ever been a victim of any anti-WHISP sentiment?"

"Until this latest role, most people didn't know I had a WHISP, so there was some fall out from that. It's sad some people think I'm like a different person now that I have a WHISP."

Hollywood Insider Interview with *Breathless WHISPer* star Jason Stone

IT IS ALL THAT I CAN DO TO WAIT UNTIL WE'RE BACK in Crone's car to give him a piece of my mind.

"So, Detective Crone, tell me, do you like cleaning up

messes made by people like Chester? Like notifying mothers their only child is dead and oh, by the way, you're gonna wanna plan for a closed casket, but you have my sincere condolences."

Crone's face turns crimson so quick it's almost like he's a cartoon character. "What do you think I was trying to do in there? I'm trying to get some fucking answers to stop these killings, not trying to buddy up with some psycho bitch!"

"You're not going to get any answers from Chester."

"Oh, right, I forgot, you're the supposed fucking Chester expert. I'm guessing you're the only person who can get answers from her then?"

I take a deep breath. This inane argument isn't helping anything either. Though I would love to blame this on Crone, it's not his fault. This whole damn debacle is actually my fault for not protesting Crone's presence to begin with. It was me being a goddamn coward and not wanting to face Chester alone, even though I knew we wouldn't get anywhere with him there. Pinching the bridge of my nose to avoid another migraine, I lighten up on Crone.

"I didn't say that. Even if she does know something, it's likely that she won't give it up. She has very little to gain. The DA's not willing to offer much in the way of deals for her cooperation due to his still being pissed about the verdicts. I hope you see I was just trying to get a little leverage with her."

Starting the car like it's personally wronged him, he grunts. "Yeah, I guess."

I try to lift the mood of failure pressing down on us. "You're aware all of her victims were men, right?"

Directing the car through the maze of exit gates, Crone grunts again, but in an amiable way. "It's weird then."

My brain's busy coming up with a strategy for when I talk to Chester alone, while simultaneously trying to come up with an excuse not to. "What's weird?"

"This copycat isn't some man-hating wench, so they're not a real copycat."

By God, the man has a point, and a good one. Glad he finally got there, but we didn't need to interview Chester to figure that out. Regardless, Crone continues.

"Probably doesn't mean dick. I'm sure the FBI has big thick files on copycats who didn't follow the original killer's MO to the letter. Most are over-obsessed wannabe murder fans trying to impress psychos, but I'm sure there's a few out there just mooching off the celebrity of the original, adding a little of their own flare to a successful formula."

"Maybe, but I'm not dismissing anything that might be close to a lead on this."

Crone chuckles. "You got a pal over at the FBI willing to help us profile this asshole?"

"Actually, I do."

———

Jeffrey isn't so much a pal as an old boyfriend. Maybe 'old booty call' is a better description, but still a good friend. I hadn't contacted him about the original Chester case because we'd had a pretty solid suspect in Chester fairly early in the case and were just waiting to track down more evidence. Despite working for the FBI for nearly ten years and being one of the few survivors of the massive 2029 nuke-it-from-space-and-salt-the-earth overhaul, Jeffrey's office is still a modest affair with a tiny window, crappy ventilation, and chairs with cracked vinyl cushions. After the preliminary hugs and queries about health and family, Jeffrey sits and takes a long swig from his coffee.

"So, Sylvy, I take it this isn't a social call."

"Well spotted. A carnal romp in your office is just a little crass, even for me."

Jeffrey sets the mug on his immaculate desk. "Jokes. Must be important."

Damn, he knows me. "Yeah, so this thing with Chester, I'm back on it."

"You're retired."

"Technically, yes, but for the next three months I'm an official consulting detective."

Jeffrey's eyebrows meet his shaggy bangs. "Like Sherlock Holmes."

"Jokes. You must not want to help me."

"Sylvy, you were a damn good cop, but this Chester thing... well it was bad for you and I was happy when you told me it was going to be your last case. This copycat is just going to drag you back into all that shit."

It was my turn to raise my eyebrows. "How did you know? The chief's supposed to have the press all bottled up."

"I got my sources."

"Well, if you know about the copycat, then you must know the victim was a woman."

"Uh huh. I take it you want a profile." Snatching a pen out of a cup of them on the corner of his desk, Jeffrey goes into his professional mode and flips open a notepad. "How close to the Chester murders was the copycat scene? A copy or a copy of a copy?"

"A copy."

"Good quality or touched up?"

"Good quality."

His pen is working a little too hard for my answers, but whatever Jeffrey's writing has brought out the cute little crease on his forehead. "Any embellishments?"

"Not that jumped out. Forensics is still combing through the place with their finest combs, but it'll take a while to sift through everything. You, uh, need details?"

"If it's as close to the Chester killings as you think it is, then no. When I heard you were on the Chester case I requisitioned the files."

I wasn't sure what to say to that. "Oh, that's...um...sweet?"

Jeffrey looks up from the pad. "Call it a mixture of professional interest and wanting to know what the hell kinda psycho my old friend was chasing."

"That's fair. Need to know anything else?"

"What's your gut saying?"

"My gut's saying that it's Chester again, only now on a woman-hating kick. I know it's impossible, but that's what's in my gut and you asked."

"Hmmm." Jeffrey scratches out a few more lines then closes his pad. "I'll get you a profile within twenty-four hours.

"Thanks."

"What does Saint Ben say about all of this?"

"He's"—my gaze shifts to the haphazard rows of books behind Jeffrey's head—"supportive."

"Bullshit."

Can't lie to Jeffrey, not well anyway, so I skirt around how bad the situation is for Ben and me. "We've come to an agreement about it."

"Uh huh. Listen, Sylvy, I don't want to sound like an ass, but do you really think your marriage with Ben is going to survive another serial killer like Chester?"

Honestly, I'm not sure it will, but walking away isn't a choice. Jeffrey has to understand that, so I'm pissed he's acting like I have one. "It's gonna have to."

CHAPTER 8

"So, you are saying that WHISPs are demons?"

"Demons, Jerry. Demons unlocked from the soul of man by technology!"

"Okay. So, if they are demons, then what, we need to exorcise them? How?"

"Like any other demon, Jerry, through faith, prayer, and the burning justice of the Lord."

Reverend Cornelius M. Salt, *The New Jerry Springer Show*, September 4th, 2031

THE MORE I POUR OVER THE EVIDENCE FROM THE new crime scene, the more I am convincing myself that no one other than Chester could have killed the woman. But that conclusion doesn't help anything, and Tina down in forensic biology is getting downright surly after my ninth call to check on the DNA processing.

"Still no DNA matches other than the victim, Detective. I'll call you if anything changes. *I'll call you.*"

Another migraine is knocking on the door of my frontal lobe, so I open the drawer of "my" desk, in actuality one that

I'm sharing with a junior detective on maternity leave, and pull out the bottle of 600mg ibuprofen I've stashed there. I pop one and wash it down with the dregs of a cold cup of coffee just as Crone saunters up looking a bit like an expectant father.

"So," he says.

"So, what?"

"So, what's the FBI have to say?"

I rub my temples. "They'll have a profile for us by tomorrow."

"Spiffy. What are we doing until then?"

So, it's we now? Interesting. I wonder what kind of bonding ritual Crone and I underwent in the past few days I'd somehow missed, but then decide he probably just wants to take partial credit for the FBI profile we're about to get.

"I'm headed home. Forensics doesn't have anything interesting yet and cyber is still looking for any e-mails, texts, etcetera they might have missed between Chester and an accomplice. So, nothing much we can do until we get the profile."

Crone parks a butt cheek on the edge of the desk and I picture the whole thing collapsing beneath his girth. "Must be nice."

I'm shutting down my laptop and packing away files into a worn, brown leather satchel Ben gave me when I made CDS. "What must be nice?"

"Getting to come and go as you please while the rest of us have to keep regular detective hours. I hope we're not paying you based on an eight-hour-a-day salary."

"Tell you what, Crone. I'll probably be up till around three in the morning going back over statements by Chester's known associates from the original investigation, so when you get up from your desk to get your 2 a.m. cuppa, why don't you give me a call?"

"Maybe I will."

I roll my eyes, not exactly at Crone, but not hiding it either. "Besides, I've just got the one case. Don't you have other cases you should be working on until this one heats up again?"

Crone dislodges himself from the desk and turns to walk away. "Again, must be nice."

———

HOURS LATER, I'M AT HOME SURROUNDED BY AN explosion of papers in the office/second bedroom when Ben gets home.

"Whoa, some thumbtacks and string, and you're a dead ringer for a conspiracy nut."

"Well, this is all starting to feel like some kind of conspiracy."

Ben winds his way to me, leans over the back of my chair, and gives me a perfunctory kiss on the lips. "Why do you say that?"

Leaning back in my chair, I crack my neck, then rest my head on his stomach. "In the original investigation, there was nothing to even remotely suggest an accomplice except for one vague witness statement from a stoned convenience store owner who thought he might have sold someone fitting Chester's description a Pepsi and a bag of Fritos during the time of one of the murders."

"And I take it there's no video footage of this transaction or a credit card receipt to verify."

"No and no. The convenience store has been taping over the same tape every night for the past 3 years, and if Chester did ever shop there, she payed cash."

"Okay, so it's a copycat then."

The rising frustration makes me lift my head. "See, that seems like the easiest answer to all this, but it's not. I can't find any communications between Chester and a fan or disciple which doesn't check out relatively harmless. I mean, she has the usual serial killer fan mail and marriage proposals, but she only corresponds with a few, and NYPD's kept tabs on all of them. Also, I can't track anything even slightly dodgy in the chain of command of any of the case files or evidence. And if someone did slip case details out the back door, they sure did a brilliant job of hiding the payout. Crone and I have been pouring through financials and no one involved in the original case had any sudden windfalls. No hospital bills of sick relatives suddenly taken care of, no new cars, boats, or vacation homes purchased, no student loans payed off, and no large cash deposits made by any immediate relatives."

"Maybe they just stashed the money under their mattress for a rainy day?"

Exhaustion takes the edge off my frustration. "I suppose it's possible, but most people don't do something as desperate and stupid as sell confidential police files for rainy day money. There are bad seeds in the department, don't get me wrong, but they're usually not also morons."

Ben gives me his thinning patience look. "So, what are you saying? That Chester somehow escaped from prison for one night to commit another murder and then snuck back into prison?"

What am I saying? My migraine rears its ugly head again. "I'm *saying* there's something we're missing."

Smacking his head with his hand, Ben opens his mouth in mock astonishment. "I've got it! Identical twins! Like in *The Prestige*."

"That's not funny."

He leans against the desk and folds his arms with a grim smile. "I know. But babe, Chester's in prison, and unless you think... It has to be an accomplice or a copycat."

I know what he was going to say. He was going to ask me if I think we convicted the wrong person, if I think Chester's innocent. I hadn't let myself really consider the possibility. All of the evidence had just fit with Chester, and I knew it in my gut it was her. She never even denied the killings until she plead not guilty in court. She'd either lived or worked or frequented each of the crime scenes, she had no solid alibis and a whole lot of hate in her, and a criminal psychologist had declared her both fit to stand trial and capable of murder in his expert opinion. Then there was the physical evidence linking her to three of the crimes. It had to be her, because if it wasn't, I'd have committed the ultimate fuck up. I'd have sent an innocent woman to jail for the rest of her life and let a killer go free.

Ben's face is consoling. I'm sure he knows what a shitty thing it was to imply, but he's right. If I don't believe the new murder was committed by an accomplice or a copycat, then it means I don't believe Chester is the original killer. And since I do believe it, I don't know why I'm making myself crazy trying to convince myself it can't be someone else doing the killing now. I hang my head in my hands, screw my eyes shut, and just breathe for a minute before answering.

"You're right. This isn't helping anything. It has to be a copycat. Something got leaked or hacked. That's the only thing that makes sense."

Ben nods. "When do you get Jeffrey's profile?"

"Tomorrow."

He takes my hand and eases me up out of the chair. "Then let's tiptoe out of here, close the door, order some Gino's pizza, watch one of your favorite Sandra Bullock movies, and forget about this until morning."

It's a tempting offer, but it's also a test. I promised Ben I could take this case without it destroying our marriage, and I don't have the excuse of a hot lead to pursue to keep me from taking a break with him tonight. Even so, it isn't easy letting him lead me out of the office and into the living room. I still feel like somewhere in the jumble of this case is a piece of the puzzle I keep overlooking and if I just go over the evidence one more time, I'll finally find it. The only reason I close the door is because I know I can sneak back in after Ben goes to sleep.

CHAPTER 9

"Why won't the principal grow a spine with this whole WHISP issue? My kids shouldn't have to go to school with kids with WHISPs. They shouldn't have teachers with WHISPs. It's ridiculous! It's like forcing them to be in the same room with a chunk of plutonium without any protection! We don't know what exposure to WHISP will do to our children! I don't want my child getting cancer from some other kid's WHISP!"

Excerpt School Board Meeting Minutes, Lincoln High School, Duluth, Minnesota

IT'S THREE A.M. AND I'M SITTING AT THE KITCHEN table with a cup of chai, filling out my therapist-mandated dream journal. I thought I'd be in my office working right now, but it seems my subconscious had other plans for me tonight. I had my usual nightmare about the night my parents were killed, only this time, Rachel Chester was there sitting on the couch in the living room waiting for me, and the faceless figure in front of the television was her WHISP. Right before I woke up chilled, sweating, and shaking, Chester spoke to it. I write the words down in the journal and underline them: <u>Sic</u> 'er, Ray.

I take another sip of tea, thinking how it would benefit greatly from some milk, but we're all out. My therapist said writing down my nightmares would help me deal with them, but for me, it's just reliving them. Trying to remember the details seems like filling in the cracks of them and making them more solid. Personally, I'd rather just try and forget. Then again, if I don't follow his advice then what's the point of going? Finished writing, I slam the journal closed. I'm not convinced there is any point. I still have nightmares, I still have trouble having a face-to-face conversation with my own son because I can't keep myself from staring at his WHISP, I still have anxiety attacks sometimes when there are too many people with WHISPs in the grocery store with me, and my life is still basically a fucking mess. The million-dollar question is: would it be worse without the therapy?

The tea isn't enough to either calm my nerves completely or keep me awake until morning, so I have to decide if I'm going to switch to chamomile or coffee. I very much do not want to go back to sleep, even if it means looking like hell tomorrow and not being sharp when we go over the profile. Coffee and work then. I French press myself a cup from a bag I bought at the coffee bar down the block, Java's Cup 'O' Joe. Though the name sounds cozy enough, there's never a line out the door and the mismatched, cushioned chairs are never filled, but the coffee's delicious and they must do a stiff trade in selling their bags of grounds to make up for their apparent lack of patronage.

I don't brew a whole pot because I don't want the aroma to wake Ben. He'd feel betrayed I went back to work after he worked so hard to give me a relaxed night off. Also, he wouldn't be able to get back to sleep and would be an unbeliev-able crabby puss tomorrow. I drift back into the office with the steaming mug and try to pick up where I left off. Four pages later, my eyes are blurry despite the coffee. I set down the papers and open my laptop. *Okay, it must be a copycat.* Even though Cyber is monitoring any Chester fan sites that pop up, I decide to check them out myself.

Sometimes Google terrifies me. When I type in "Rachel Chester fan club," I get over ten-thousand hits. *There is no way that Cyber can be monitoring even a fraction of this shit.* I go to page twenty and click on the top website, man-hater.net. Many of the individuals posting on this site are praising Chester for having the balls and the strength to murder men who obviously had it coming for one reason or another. All of the chatter is bland and generic with many, "I wish I could…" and "my boss better watch out or I'll…" statements, but none give any specifics that earmark them as real threats, so I move on.

The next few sites are similar. Then I'm down to murder-whisp.com and my finger is hovering over the touchscreen. *Just skip to the next one.* But I can't. The words of Dr. Fritz echo in my ears, 'Avoidance of a phobia is not helpful.' My heart already racing, I touch the link. The screen goes white as the loading bar races across the top, then I'm staring into the featureless face of a WHISP holding a bloody knife. My throat goes dry and blood pounds in my ears. Seconds march by before I come to my senses. WHISPs can't hold knives. The picture is photo-shopped, and there's a bunch of them. WHISPs strangling people, WHISPs with scythes wearing hooded cloaks, WHISPs brandishing machetes and sporting hockey masks, WHISPs pulling people underwater to drown; the coup de grâce, Rachel Chester's WHISP "Ray" kneeling in the guts of a dismembered man.

———

"You look like shit. Guess you weren't lying about being up until three a.m."

I don't dignify Crone with a response. Jeffrey's profile came and I'm busy printing us out copies. It's only a page long, which surprises me. Handing Crone his copy, I'm already skimming. According to the FBI, the victim being Caucasian indicated the killer was most likely Caucasian themselves. The mutilation of the victim suggested the killer suffers from schizophrenia or some other mental illness, though the killer may not show obvious signs of this mental instability. The lack of apparent planning of the crime suggested a perpetrator of only average intelligence, but lack of evidence at the crime scene spoke of an individual with at least a modest understanding of forensics.

Based on the absence of theft or sexual assault, and the absence of obvious criminal background, extreme religion, or strong political affiliation, etc. of the victim, the motivation of the killer is likely either hedonistic thrill or a desire to control. Since hedonistic thrill seekers tended to be younger while individuals desiring control over their victims tended to be older, the FBI chose to default to the standard average serial killer age of 29 years. Copycat killers tended to follow gender lines, so it was likely the copycat was a woman, as well. The last bit of information was, the killer was likely someone with an unappreciated job or life position who's seeking attention through association with Rachel Chester, but not necessarily someone who's obsessed with Rachel Chester.

I've never read an FBI profile before, but movies have led me to believe profilers were near wizards who could narrow down things like height, weight, hair color, and ice cream preference, so this seems pretty weak.

"Well that's useless. So glad you pulled strings with the FBI for generic bullshit."

Disappointed as I am, I'm not about to give Crone the satisfaction. "Actually, I think it narrows down things quite a bit. We're looking for a Caucasian woman in her late twenties to early thirties who is good at hiding a mental illness and relatively well-off but feels bored and unappreciated. She's not a planner, so she doesn't stalk her victims, therefore we're likely looking for an opportunist. Chester's been in prison for a month now, so either it took that long for the copycat to get the information to mimic the murders, or she just got free from an obligation which was taking up her free time until now, or maybe some inciting event set off her latent mental illness just recently."

Crone's gaping mouth makes him look suspiciously like a largemouth bass.

"Screw the FBI, next time just do the damn profile yourself."

Rolling my eyes, I try not to let Crone's "flattery" go to my head. "Don't thank me yet. An opportunist is going to be impossible to predict, and if she's not really a Chester fan, but just riding the publicity train, then Cyber's wasting their time."

He shrugs. "Not necessarily. They may spot other wannabe celebrities, and who knows, maybe since the press isn't on to the copycat yet, she might go online to brag on one of those serial killer club sites."

I nod. "Good point. God, wouldn't that be nice?"

CHAPTER 10

"Well folks, if you were hoping to move to Greenland to escape the WHISP phenomenon, I've got some bad news for you. Yesterday, researchers confirmed the first case of a WHISP in Nuuk."

CBS News at Eleven

"HARBINGER, SADDLE UP, WE'VE CAUGHT A BREAK!"

From the way my head dips off my hand, I can tell that I've been dozing at my desk again, sleep still being an elusive and fickle thing in my life. As I wipe away some drool, I try to play off my sluggishness as having been deeply focused on the files on my desk, and shuffle them around accordingly. "What's that?"

Crone toddles in, winded and red-faced but smiling. "We found a link from our vic to a disgruntled ex-boyfriend with a long list of priors."

"So?"

"So, the boyfriend has a WHISP and, get this, before he started dating Petrie, he was court-ordered to go to a WHISP support group for anger management. Guess who also attended the same WHISP support group?"

"Rachel fucking Chester."

"Damn right, and we've got uniforms watching his digs. He just got home from work."

I get up and grab my coat. "Not nearly enough for a warrant even, and any evidence we can link to him from Alice's apartment, he'll just say was there from when they were dating. We can't even bring him in for questioning if he doesn't agree."

As we head toward the elevator, Crone reaches into his pocket and produces a folded piece of paper. "Oh, ye of little faith. Maybe he should've paid his parking tickets in a little more timely fashion."

"You're kidding me."

"Nope, we can hold him until the bench warrant gets sorted."

"Perfect. I'll drive."

———

ON THE WAY TO THE BOYFRIEND'S BRONX ADDRESS, I catch Crone glancing at me, a sly gleam in his eyes.

"What?"

"You didn't ask me what the boyfriend's name is."

"Okay, what is it?"

"Stan Trentwood."

My brow creases. "Stan Trentwood. Why does that name sound so familiar?"

Crone is giddy. "Maybe because you've arrested him before."

"What?"

"Yeah, a couple of years ago he was a suspect in the murder of a liquor store owner. He'd robbed the store, but turned out the ex-wife shot the guy and tried to make it look like a robbery gone bad."

Vague memories float around in my head. It wasn't a very memorable case, and he hadn't had a WHISP then.

"Huh, small world."

In the passenger seat, Crone sulks. I guess he expected more of a reaction out of me, but I've arrested a lot of people in the city, and, unfortunately, Trentwood's not the only one I will have arrested twice. Soon, we're pulling up in front of a run-down grey house with what used to be a brown Chevy Impala parked in the driveway, the vehicle now a conglomerate of mottled brown, rust, and replacement panels.

"Wanna dismiss the uni?"

Parking the car on the street, I shake my head. "Nah, if he tries to flee, best if we have back-up."

Crone unbuckles his seatbelt. "Fair enough."

After I radio the uniformed officer parked in a patrol car a block down the street, Crone and I get out of the car and head up the driveway toward the house. Instinctively, I watch for any movement either from inside the house or near the rear. Next to me, Crone is also on alert, though if the suspect made a break for it, I'm not sure Crone would be able to give chase for more than a block before he collapsed. Internally, I snicker. *And he wanted me to send the uni away*. At the door, Crone presses the doorbell, which then falls off the wall and exposes a small hole with rusted out wiring inside. As Crone stares down at the bell, I knock.

"NYPD! Open up!"

From inside comes the sound of movement, but no one comes to the door.

I pull my gun. "I'll go cover the back."

As I round the side of the house, Crone is knocking again.

"NYPD! We have a warrant for the arrest of Stanley Trentwood!"

There's a chain-link fence blocking access to the back of the house, but when I get closer to it, I spy a man running through the backyard. He fits what I remember of Stan, about six-seven, Italian skin-tone, black hair, and he has a WHISP.

"Stop! I'm armed and I will shoot!"

Stan doesn't slow, but instead busts through a gap in the back-neighbor's privacy fence.

"Shit!"

Using my free hand to help propel me over, I run up and hop the low fence, hitting the ground running on the other side. "Crone, he's running! Call it in!"

I sprint to the gap in the fence, but slow and lead with my gun as I make my way through the gap. Scanning the yard on the other side, I don't see Trentwood, but there are two little girls on a set of swings. When they see me, they both point to my right and I spot him fleeing across the next yard.

"Thanks."

My side starts to stitch with pain as I take off after him again. Fortunately, the fence on this side of the yard is in the middle of repairs and only halfway complete, so I don't have to leap over it. Sadly, Trentwood is headed toward a taller, wooden fence on the far side of the next yard that I'm not sure I'm going to be able to scale. Since I can't risk hitting more children on the other side of the fence, I can only hope to get to him before he makes it over and drag him down. I put on a burst of speed, but my stylish, yet sensitive, flats aren't all that great for running over wet grass. He jumps, seizes the top of the fence, pulls himself up, and gets a leg over. *I'm not going to make it.*

"Stop!" I reach the fence and snatch at Trentwood's ankle, but my fingers only brush his sock. "Dammit!"

I'm already running along the fence again looking for an opening, when I hear the barking and snarling of a large dog and a man screaming for help. *Shit.* I reach the corner of the fence line, overturn a garbage can and clamber on it to get over top of the fence. On the other side, Trentwood is on the ground, one bloody pant leg in the jaws of a Rottweiler, his WHISP writhing next to him.

I bang on the fence to get the dog's attention. "Hey! Hey Doggie!"

The dog doesn't respond, but Trentwood looks up at me. "Shoot it!"

"I'm not going to shoot a dog for protecting its own yard, asshole." Balancing myself, I radio Crone. "It's me. Suspect is one street behind and one house over, a green two story with lighter green trim. We may need animal control."

———

TURNS OUT WE DON'T NEED ANIMAL CONTROL. THE owner, a recent immigrant from Cambodia, was taking a nap, and once roused by Crone pounding on her door, she is able to call off the dog, Bolla, whilst we corralled and handcuffed a traumatized Trentwood. After paramedics bandage his leg and we double check the dog's rabies vaccination papers, the uniform, Officer Saunders, transports Trentwood back to the precinct for us. Getting there just a few minutes before them, I have time to map out an interrogation strategy with Crone. Not long after, he and I sit facing Trentwood in the interrogation room.

Trentwood is twitchy and fidgeting, and it's hard not to get distracted by his WHISP as it shimmies and ripples behind him. Casually, Crone opens Trentwood's file and begins paging through it.

"Hooboy, Stan, I can see why you tried to bolt. You've got quite the record here. Let's see, we've got some B and E's, some assaults, a grand theft auto, and now there's this matter with your unpaid parking tickets."

Stan's eyebrows knit. "Wait. This is about my parking tickets? You chased me, threatened to shoot me, and got me mauled by a rockwilder, for some fucking parking tickets? What's wrong with you people?"

"What's wrong with us? What's wrong with you, Stan? Why can't you seem to obey the law for five minutes?"

Shaking his head, Stan leans back in his chair. "You're all crazy. And I do what I gotta do to get by."

"Interesting, is there anything you had to do the other night you want to tell us about?"

"Nope. I've seen a bunch of Law and Order and I'm just gonna sit here and wait for my court-appointed lawyer." Trentwood sets his jaw and leans back in his chair.

That's my cue. "Actually, I noticed something very interesting about one of those parking tickets."

Crone's eyebrows lift as his eyes widen. "Oh, Detective Harbinger, and what was that?"

"One of them was within four blocks of Alice Petrie's apartment the night of her murder."

"You don't say."

I nod. "Since Stan dated the victim, I bet it's enough to get a warrant for his house."

"Wait, wait, wait, you don't think I had something to do with Alice's…with what happened to Alice?"

Crone ticks points off his fingers as he says, "You're a scumbag, she broke it off with you, you decided to take a page out of your good buddy Rachel Chester's notebook and teach her a lesson. Motive, opportunity, it's all there."

Stan's eyes tear up and he wipes at them with the backs of his cuffed hands. "That's just fucked up. I loved that girl. I would never have hurt her, and I don't even know Rachel Chester."

Leaning forward, I smack a hand down on the table. "Cut the sad boyfriend act, Stan, you both went to the same WHISP support group."

"What? No we didn't."

I produce a photocopy of a sign-in sheet from the group and slide it toward him. Stan's name is four names down from Chester's. He stares at it with his mouth hanging open and then looks up and pushes the paper back at me.

"That wasn't me."

"Funny, looks like your name right there is black and white, four names down from Chester." I lift the paper and hold it in front of Crone. "Doesn't it look like his name, Crone?"

Crone scrutinizes the page and nods. "It really does."

Stan's eyes dart back and forth between us. Sweating now, his breaths are shallow with panic. "No, I mean, yeah, that's my name, but it ain't me. It wasn't me. I didn't wanna go to some retarded meeting, but the judge said I had to, so I paid a buddy of mine to go for me. He also got a WHISP. It's not like they check ID at a group therapy session, so all he had to do was sign my name."

"That's a pretty convenient story, Stan."

"It's true, you can even ask him. His name's Benny, Benny J. I paid him twenty dollars. Check it. Or better yet, do one of those handwriting thingy things y'all do. It ain't gonna match."

Peeking over at Crone, I can tell he's pissed. If Stan's story is true, then we've got no connection from Stan to Chester. We've got nothing.

"Oh, don't worry, we'll check."

CHAPTER 11

WHISP21: U get spit on yet?

WhIsP447: No, but had 2 chnge #, 2 many dth thrts

WHISP21: Wlcme 2 the club

Twitter posts, December 2030

THE NEXT DAY I'M TRYING NOT TO THROW THINGS because Trentwood's alibi Benny J. checked out.

"Detective Harbinger?"

I glance up at a perky blonde officer and have an irrational desire to smack the grin off her face. "Hmmm."

"You have a phone call on line two."

"Thank you."

She flounces away and my mood isn't improved. Expecting a cranky Ben wondering when I'm going to be home for dinner, I lift the receiver with two fingers and almost just say hello before I catch myself. "Detective Harbinger."

There's silence for a few seconds, then a wavering voice pushes through the line. "Yeah, hi, um, you ah, were the detective on the Chester case."

The caller doesn't sound like someone from the press. "Yes, one of them. Who, may I ask, is calling?"

"Oh, I thought I recognized you. I, ah, I'd thought you'd retired, but then I saw you at the station after…"

"I've been brought back into the NYPD to consult for a short time. What can I do for you?"

The caller clears their throat. "Um, I, ah, saw something… the other night, when my neighbor, Alice Petrie, was…killed."

The mysterious caller has my full attention now. Sounds like a male, older, forties maybe? I check the phone for recording and tapping capabilities, nada. "I'm sorry, what was your name again, sir?"

"Oh, I, ah, prefer not to…it's just…what I saw was, um, odd, and I, ah, don't want you to think I'm some kind of crack pot or anything…but um, you can call me, ah, Mike."

"Okay, Mike, what did you see?"

His sigh whistles through the receiver. "I saw a WHISP."

This is huge. If the killer has a WHISP, that narrows down the pool of suspects considerably. "Are you sure?"

"Positive."

"So, you saw a person with a WHISP at your neighbor's, on the night she was killed. What did they look like?"

"Ah…no…ah…you don't understand. It wasn't a person with a WHISP, it was just a WHISP all by itself. I know it sounds crazy. That's why I didn't come forward before. But I had to tell somebody, and then I saw you and then people say that you have a thing about WHISPs so then I thought if anyone would believe me, it would be you."

Goddamn that reporter. During the trial, one snot-nosed reporter got wind of my therapy, snooped around for gossip and somehow found out about my aversion to WHISPs. She'd written a scathing article about society's bias against people with WHISPs, how they were the new oppressed minority… and mentioned me being the lead detective on Chester's case.

Now everybody and their brother's son's soccer coach knew I didn't like WHISPs.

"Okay, Mike, just slow down. Start from the beginning. What time did you see something?"

"It was around three in the morning and I got up to go to the bathroom, and I just happened to look out the hallway window, I don't know why, but then I saw this like flash in Alice's window and then I saw the WHISP, all by itself. I know it was alone because the window's pretty big and it walked in front of the window but no one was walking in front of it. Anyways, then I couldn't see anything anymore, and I couldn't remember if she had a WHISP, and then I thought maybe I was kinda still dreaming, 'cause I ate some bad sushi and that's why I was getting up in the first place. But then I saw the police cars later that morning and I knew something bad had happened to her...well, I didn't *know*, know, I couldn't *know*, but I had a feeling, and then I wanted to tell someone about the WHISP, but then I got scared and..."

Probably the poor guy was just having severe food poisoning dehydration visions. WHISPs weren't living things, they were like shadows, shadows made of magnetic waves and crap instead of light, but shadows nonetheless. They couldn't walk around by themselves, let alone kill someone. Yet, just because the guy didn't see a person through the window didn't mean there wasn't one, so the lead could still be good. It was just a matter of getting him talking and not spooking him.

"What did it look like?"

"What do you mean? It was a WHISP."

"I mean, was it tall or short? Male or female? Fat or thin? Did it have any distinctive characteristics, perhaps from the clothing of its person?"

"Oh, I...uh...maybe it was more woman-shaped, not real tall. It wasn't all that skinny...but not fat either...I can't think of anything that stood out too much."

"Mike, are you sure that you don't want to come down and give an official statement? Maybe work with a sketch artist? I promise we will take everything you say seriously."

"Nah...I...there isn't really anything else. I'm not sure about exactly what it looked like because I was too freaked out by it being all by itself. At least it really looked... Anyways, I was too tired to notice much, but I know what I saw, and I just thought you needed to know."

"You might remember more details if you meet with one of our sketch artists. They're really good at getting people to remember little details. Maybe she'll even help you remember seeing a person, too."

"Wait, a person? You believe me, don't you Detective? I mean, you know WHISPs are bad, right?"

For a detective, I'm not the world's greatest liar. I had a little rapport with this guy, but I wasn't willing to go all in with him and find out he was with some damn WHISPs rights group and recording our whole conversation. It was about the last thing I needed right now.

"I know you saw something, Mike, and I really would like for you to tell me more about it. Please, just come in and we can get everything straight."

"Oh my God, you don't believe me. I thought you, of all people. I... Fuck..."

The line clicked and went dead.

Fuck.

CHAPTER 12

Status?
Five anomalies observed and two collected for observation, one lost.
Risk assessment?
Unknown.
Prediction of repetition of anomaly?
100%
Recommendation?
Containment and study.
Outcome of loss?
Eradication of anomaly.

Department of Energy WHISP report hacked and publicized by Anonymous

"So, how reliable do you think this Mike lead is? He sounds like a whack job." Crone picked through the doughnut box on the breakroom table and selected a big fat bear claw.

"Well, obviously he didn't see a WHISP walking around by itself, but if he saw a WHISP, then it means the killer has a

WHISP. Narrows down our suspect pool." I choose a French crueler.

Swallowing a massive bite he barely chewed, Crone frowns. "Yeah, maybe, but he might not of seen anything but his own reflection for all we know, or the victim's WHISP. She had one right?"

I nod.

"So, we could be barking up the wrong tree entirely going after WHISPers."

"Hey Detective." A clean-cut officer with dark brown hair is making his way across the sea of desks toward the breakroom. His name is Gary Waller and he's a damn fine cop. He'd been a first responder to my cases before and I trusted him to clear a building without contaminating a crime scene. There's just one problem; his daughter has a WHISP and he thinks I'm a prejudiced asshole. We exchanged words at a WHISP sensitivity training two years ago. I have no idea what he's doing here.

"Hello, Officer Waller. I thought you'd switched to working graveyard."

Waller smiles but it's a hard smile and devoid of friendliness. "I heard you were back to work in the precinct and I changed my mind."

I raise an eyebrow. *Did he really just say that he switched shifts to check up on me?*

"Or, I just swapped shifts with a buddy this week."

Waller is blocking Crone in the breakroom, sizing him up. Though I'm sorely tempted not to introduce the two, I try to be the better person.

"Officer Gary Waller, this is Detective Lieutenant Crone." It occurs to me then that I've been working with Crone for two weeks now and don't even know his first name. *Huh.*

The two men trade grips with a fair amount of thinly veiled male posturing.

"Officer."

"Lieutenant."

Clearing my throat, I attempt to cut through the tension. "So, what brings you up here?"

"Thought I'd save you a trip." Waller hands me a file.

I flick it open and see that it's the report on Alice Petrie's cell phone with all recent activity for the past few weeks. I'd had some junior detectives cross-reference her records with the records of Chester's victims and few known associates on the off chance we'd find a connection. The report hadn't found a connection, but it did note the cell phone company had mentioned an irregularity with her cell phone signal the night of her murder.

"Anything helpful?" Waller is peeking over the top of the folder. He's too strait-laced to have read the report before handing it over to me, but it doesn't mean he trusts how I'm handling the case.

I close it. "Sorry, not really, but thanks for the effort and stopping by to say 'howdy.'"

"Well, sorry it didn't break the case. I'm sure I'll see you around."

Translation: I'm watching you.

"Thanks for the report."

Waller gives one last long look, probably meant to intimidate me, then stalks off.

"Are you gonna let me see that?" Crone, either oblivious or ignoring Waller, sets down his jelly doughnut.

"Sure." I hand the folder over to his sticky fingers. "They didn't find any connections, but the cell company said something weird was going on with her phone the night of her murder. Something about a power surge and service interruption. That can be caused by being in close proximity to a WHISP right? I guess Mr. Mike really did see a WHISP."

Crone licks red jelly off his index finger as he reads through the report. "Guess so, but again, could've just been due to her own WHISP." He gives me a sidelong glance. I'm sure he's heard more than a few rumors racing around the precinct regarding me and WHISPs. "This isn't going to turn into another WHISP issue media circus shitstorm, is it?"

My jaw tightens. "I don't control the media."

"Well, maybe try not to give them as much to sink their teeth into this time."

I turn on my heel and leave the breakroom before I punch him in the face.

———

IT ISN'T CLEAR TO ME JUST HOW TIGHT I AM stretched until we get a call later that day and I snap. There'd been another copycat murder. The shock I feel is ridiculous. I'd known this was coming, yet the news still crashes down on me and makes it hard to breathe. My insides are burning with anger and shame. I want to cry, I want to throw things, I want to run away and hide, I want to hit someone; what I don't want to do is go to another Chester-inspired crime scene. *Keep it together*. Breathing in and then out slowly, counting in my head, I reconstruct my wall.

I have to go to the crime scene. Seeing it with my own eyes is the only way I can be sure I don't see something no one else does. I can't leave the task to others and risk missing something. Plus, going to the crime scene is a form of psychological punishment, according to my therapist, for not catching the killer before they struck again. A punishment my gut is telling me is fair while my brain is telling me I did everything I could to prevent another murder. One of them is a liar.

The victim is an eighty-six-year-old woman and before I even find out the victim's name, I know something is different. Previous victims have all been under the age of fifty. Then we get an ID and I feel the room spinning around me. I have to grip the desk to keep steady. Pamela Sistern is a name I recognize. She was Rachel Chester's landlady for a brief period several years ago. I interviewed her just before we arrested Chester. The interview is very clear in my mind because the woman had a WHISP. Though extremely rare for people over sixty to have them, Ms. Sistern was a technophile and even claimed to be one of the first people to have a WHISP. She hadn't named hers like Chester had, but fondly referred to it as her "shadow."

Sistern wasn't the kindly old grandmother type. She was hard and sharp as old peanut brittle, though softened when she spoke of Chester. She said in the interview, Rachel seemed lonely, but at least had "Ray" to keep her company, like her "shadow" did for her. When I asked her to comment on whether she thought Chester capable of murdering those six men, Sistern replied that every human on earth was capable of murder. The interview hadn't really gone anywhere useful, but at one point I'd stepped out to take a breather and was chatting with the chief behind the two-way mirror of the interrogation room when Sistern did something creepy. Looking over her shoulder at her WHISP, she had spoken to it. Not just spoken to it, she'd had a whole whispered conversation with it. Just recalling the moment makes my spine stiffen and stomach knot.

But what has me reeling right now is, Sistern hadn't given us any evidence against Chester, and seemed to like her. She hadn't even been at the trial. None of the other victims, original or copycat, had such an obvious tie to Chester. I don't know whether this means anything or not, whether it will help us catch the copycat or just confuse the case even more. Maybe the copycat really wasn't a fan of Chester and just saw Pamela Sistern had given a statement to NYPD and then assumed something in the statement led to Chester's arrest. Or maybe the copycat hadn't gotten the publicity she wanted by killing a random person with Chester's MO, so she'd decided to kill someone who knew Chester as a bid for more attention.

My head is still spinning in Crone's car on the way to the new crime scene. Crone is unexpectedly and blissfully silent on the drive. I don't know if he's thinking about a lot of the same questions I am or if he's just stewing because the killer had struck again with us still being mostly in the dark. When we pull up, the front of the boarding-house-slash-apartment-complex is littered with media vans.

"Shit."

I think Crone has summed things up quite succinctly, so I say nothing. But I know at least one thing before I open the car door, if the copycat was looking for notoriety, she got it with this victim. We fight our way through, and have barely finished with the coroner when my cell rings and then Crone's rings a split second later. *What the hell?* The phone feels cold against my cheek.

"Harbinger."

"Detective, there's been another."

CHAPTER 13

"And lo the angel came and wept by Saint Gregory's side, saying, 'See what man hath done with the freedom granted unto him by God. He has sundered himself in twain, and hath pushed his own soul from his body and then shunned it.'"

Gospel of WHISP 20:17

It's seven in the morning and I've been at the precinct all night. Ben had brought me some egg rolls and moo shu pork around eleven with only a hint of martyrdom on his face. I'd done my best to turn off from the case for the few moments he was there, but it was too much, and the case was too fresh. He'd seen it in my eyes and didn't linger. Now I was calling the sad, reheated leftovers breakfast.

Two murders. Same copycat MO, different ends of the city, and the coroner can't appreciably differentiate times of death. One, Pamela Sistern, an eighty-six-year-old female known associate of Chester; the other, William Rocks, a twenty-two-year-old male accountant with no obvious ties to Chester or previous victims. It didn't take long for the words "cult following" to make their way around the precinct. I couldn't swallow it. Rachel Chester being responsible for fostering a cult just didn't compute. She liked to get into people's heads, sure, but cult leaders had charm, charisma. Compared to David Koresh, Rachel Chester was a dead fish.

The chief knocks on the corner of my desk. I hadn't noticed him walk up.

"I've got some news."

From the tilt of his mouth, it's not news I'm going to be happy with.

"I've called in the FBI."

Maybe before the Chester case I'd have fought the chief tooth and nail on this, but right now, all I do is nod. I don't want to answer to some dick in a black suit, but I also had my shot at cracking this case solo. Ego will only get more people killed and then even more blood would be on my hands.

"They'll be here for a briefing at nine. Maybe you want to go home and change...maybe take a shower? For the sake of the rest of us?"

Despite everything, a weak smile manages to move the corner of my lips. "For you, Sir. Screw the FBI and everyone else."

Home and back in record time, in clean clothes and smelling of eucalyptus stress-relief body wash, I'm one of the first people in the briefing room. A younger agent with neat, brown hair is setting up a screen and hooking a laptop to a projector. He glances up when I pull out a chair, recognition flashing in his eyes. Straightening, he winds around the table and holds out his hand to me.

"Agent Coppola."

I stand to shake his hand. "Detective Lieutenant Harbinger."

"I thought so, but I thought..."

"Thought I retired? So did I. I'm just back for three months as a consultant on the Chester copycat."

"You mean cult."

Not really, but I don't want to antagonize Agent Coppola within the first two minutes of meeting him. "I honestly hope not."

Agent Coppola's gaze takes on an appraising quality. "All right, what's your take then?"

"Don't really have one yet, but my gut's telling me it isn't a cult. Cult leaders have charisma. I've met Rachel Chester, she doesn't."

"Doesn't mean one of her fans lacks charisma or she didn't have an accomplice with charisma."

So now we're back from cults to accomplices, and I can feel the muscles in my jaw locking up. "Chester's only accomplice is Ray."

One chestnut eyebrow raises. "Her WHISP?"

Instantly, I regret saying something so stupid. I'm trying to get people to dismiss rumors of me being on some kind of crazy crusade against WHISPs. Smiling, I layer my reply with sarcasm, "It was a joke, Agent Coppola."

"Right. Sorry. My sense of humor is always a bit stunted in the face of two dead bodies and a possible cu—possibility of more than one killer on the loose."

Tired as I am, I'm not in any mood to take sanctimonious bullshit from this fed. "Christ, you know I didn't mean it like that. No one's had to see more of Chester's legacy of horror than I have, Agent. I was just trying to make a point. I don't see her having an accomplice or a cult following, it doesn't make sense. We're missing something."

Agent Coppola opens his mouth, but a stream of people flows into the room, and he has a briefing to run. He turns and strides back behind the table and up to the podium. Irritation stoked by exhaustion is making me too twitchy to sit right away. I feel like I need an ally. Instead, a well-rested Crone shuffles in and regards Agent Coppola with a glower. Unfortunately, images of him and Coppola in a literal pissing contest fill my weary mind. Trying very hard to dispense mental bleach, I approach Crone.

"Funny, he doesn't look like the chief." I cock my thumb toward Coppola.

Crone huffs. "This is bullshit. We ask them for a profile and suddenly the feds think they own our fucking case."

"Oh, so this is my fault and not the near simultaneous pair of homicides last night."

His glower turning into more of an amused pout, he amends his statement, "Someone mentions the word cult and suddenly the feds think they own our fucking case."

"Better."

We sit together in feigned indignant solidarity. Crone might actually be slightly pissed off at the feds taking over the investigation, but deep down he doesn't want more people to die, either. At least, I hope that's the case, I still don't know the man's first name. We sit silently amidst the milling and murmuring until the clock on the wall strikes nine and Agent Coppola calls the briefing to order.

"All right folks, this is what we know..."

My rapt attention at Coppola's words steadily wanes as he repeats information that I've been going over all night. My mind drifts and I catch myself dozing off despite my anxiety and frayed nerves. Going over the conversation with Coppola again in my head, I'm mad I let him get to me, but even angrier I didn't have a workable theory about the murders to replace the FBI's cult or maybe multiple accomplices scenarios. Both seem overly complicated. Murder is hard and messy. It has to be a trick for a single killer to butcher their victims the same way every time, let alone getting multiple killers to cut up a body the exact same way. Occam's razor comes to mind, but I can't come up with the simple explanation for the life of me.

Coppola saying my name drags me from my reverie.

"…has agreed to suspend her retirement briefly in order to consult on this case. For anyone living under a rock for the past year, Detective Harbinger was the lead detective on the original Rachel Chester case. Direct any questions regarding the original murders to her."

Crone surreptitiously elbows me in the ribs.

"Now, we have to remember, even though these murders are very similar to those committed by Chester, this is a *different* killer or killers. They are murdering women as well as men. Also, one of the victims knew Rachel Chester personally, which is unique from Chester's original victims. Her only living relatives are her mother who lives in a nursing home in Queens and a cousin who resides in Covina, California. We've already stationed officers to monitor Chester's mother and the FBI is working with Los Angeles police to place a detail on the cousin, but we can't rely on them being the killer's next targets. There's been escalation and we don't want to see any more bodies. But we need to be fast and efficient. I'll be handing out assignments, but if you feel like you can take on more than I give you, I've got more than enough for everyone. Work smart, work together, and keep the lines of communication open. Questions?"

"How many members do you think are in this cult?"

Coppola shakes his head. "We haven't found any evidence yet to support the cult following theory other than the impossibility for yesterday's murders to have been committed by the same person. So, to answer your question, if it is a cult, at least two."

Low laughter trills through the room.

The fed's mouth remains a tight, humorless line. "Any other questions?"

"Yeah, what does Chester have to say about all this?"

My face burns and my molars grind.

"She didn't have anything to say after the first copycat murder, but she might now that Pamela Sistern is dead." Coppola directs the glare of his tan eyes right on me. "Which is why Detective Harbinger has offered to interview her again."

CHAPTER 14

"There is a clear scientific explanation for WHISPs. They are comprised of clouds of magnetically charged particles that orbit the electricity generated by the human body, and this is why their appearance resembles a "shadow" of static electricity. Particles of this nature have no anima, they are no more alive than the electron clouds around the nuclei of atoms."

Dr. Harold Lieber, PhD, Particle Physics, King's College, London

I WAS GOING TO INTERVIEW CHESTER AGAIN ANYWAY, but Coppola making it seem like it was his idea pisses me off to no end. As soon as he dismisses us, I'm out of my seat and storming to my desk. I've got my car keys out of the drawer when Crone appears, puffing like The Little Engine that Could, and grabs my shoulder.

"You're not going to see Chester right now."

"No, I'm not."

He releases me. "Oh."

"Give me a little credit, Crone. I know when I'm tapped out. If I go like this she'll eat me alive and I'll come out with jack shit. I'm gonna go home, get about four hours of sleep and then take another shot at her."

Crone rubs his neck. "I should go with you."

Shutting the desk drawer with more force than I mean to, I meet his gaze. "We both know that's not true, so please don't do anything stupid like try to appeal to the chief."

I didn't anticipate the injured look on Crone's face, but it only lasts a heartbeat before his usual swagger is back. "Give *me* a little credit. I know you're the chief's pet detective. Just, you know...don't fuck it up."

The sentimentality of his words actually produces a twinge in my chest.

———

"HELL NO, YOU'RE NOT!"

For the nth time I'm regretting telling Ben about going to see Chester again, only alone this time. To be fair, I was operating on four hours of Benedryl-induced sleep followed by a slammed off-brand energy drink when he asked me why I had to leave the apartment.

"This is crazy! Why can't someone go with you?"

I'm slipping on my second shoe, while balancing on the other foot and trying not to break my ankle. Black pants, black blazer, white blouse, and black heels: battle armor. "Because she won't talk if someone else is there."

"You don't know that. I'm not saying you need to take Crone, just somebody, anybody else."

Both shoes now on, I'm searching for my car keys. "Another person would just be a distraction. Two more people are dead. I can't just fuck around because Chester gives me the willies."

He grabs my arm. "Sylvy, love, you don't have to do this. I know you think you do, but you don't."

"Ben, I already have blood on my hands because I let Crone come with me the first time. I do have to do this."

We stare at each other in silence.

"You need to let me do this."

Ben grinds his teeth. "Like hell I do."

"A month, Ben. You promised me a month."

Something which isn't quite resignation takes hold in his eyes. Letting me go, he reaches into his pocket and pulls out my car keys.

———

THE SLANTING, LATE AFTERNOON SUN DOES NOTHING to cheer up the exterior of Rikers Island. It's later than it should be for an inmate interview, but the FBI pulled some strings so I'm not on any fixed schedule except for the countdown going on in my head, the one that will hit zero when the copycat or copycats or cult or whateverthefuck strikes again. Chester isn't waiting for me when I get to the interrogation room, but is brought in about ten minutes later in full cuffs and chains by two guards. The guards sit her in the metal chair that is bolted to the floor and then lock her leg cuffs to a ring set in the floor and her wrist cuffs to a ring in the table. My eyes are focused on Chester, but the way the guards secure her forces her to sit up straight and makes Ray visible to me over her shoulder. One of the guards nearly walks through the WHISP as they both retreat toward the door and take up positions on either side.

Right away, I sense that Chester isn't as collected as she typically is. Normally, even chained, she exhibits a laziness in the way she carries herself, but not now. There's tension in her limbs even though her face is slack, and an odd mark at the corner of her eye stands out. It wasn't there when I interviewed her with Crone.

"What, no monkey this time? Pity. It was pretty funny watching him trying to fling his feces at me."

"You should see him smoke a cigarette while riding a unicycle. But I wanted a chat without distractions today, just the two of us."

The corner of Chester's mouth flicks up. "No, you didn't, but you thought it would help. Cute." She blinks and the injured eye twitches, the left one. Her sclera is red just on the side with the mark.

I rub my own left eye. "Ah, sorry about that, had an itch. Pink eye must be a bitch with those cuffs on."

"Oh, I wouldn't worry about my eye. It was just a...misunderstanding, but it's all cleared up now."

A misunderstanding? Did one of the guards do it? Even if it's Chester, that's not even a little bit okay. I check the guards' faces for a reaction, but they aren't looking at us or even hardly blinking. "Rachel, there shouldn't be any misunderstandings in here. Not anymore. If someone hurt you—"

Chester laughs long and loud, letting her mask of humanity fall away and revealing the cold, dangerous thing I know lives underneath. "You remind me of a hamster I had once, Detective. Bert was fun to play with until he bit me. Did you know hamsters can scream when you put them in the garbage disposal? It's a unique sound. You wouldn't think something so small could make it."

Okay, so probably not abuse from a guard. *Focus, Harbinger.* "Threats from you are kinda less scary when you're chained to a chair. Makes me think you think I should be afraid though. Interesting."

Chester lunges across the table toward me. "Fool!"

I was expecting some kind of reaction, so it isn't her movement that makes me jump, but coming face to not-face with Ray. The guards reach Chester in seconds. One grips her around the throat with a baton and the other stands well clear and unsheathes his stun gun.

"Chester, this is your warning! Relax or I'm lighting you up."

Crap. I was too reckless. I could see she was off kilter and I pushed too hard too fast. FBI influence or not, the interview is over.

"I think you should be afraid." Foamy spit is accumulating at the corners of Chester's mouth and raining down onto the table. Her eyes flick to the side like she's trying to look over her shoulder and I wonder if she's trying to get a bead on the guard behind her.

I'm out of time, but I take one last shot. "How many?"

"How many what?"

"How many disciples?"

I'm expecting a sneer, a last insult, Chester to spit in my face; what I'm not expecting is the complete confusion in her eyes.

"Out of the way, Detective! Jones, get clear! Barthel three forty-nine discharging weapon in three, two…"

Chester's shoulders are slumping as she retreats into her head and a blankness spreads through her eyes. Her injured eye spasms. In another few seconds she'd be docile again, but the guard with the stun gun doesn't give her that long. The gun's barbs hit Chester in the chest and she jerks like a speared fish then drops as far as the chains will allow. Behind her, Ray is slouching, but suspended in mid-air, her head, like Chester's, tilted slightly toward me. Chester's eyes are closed, but I can't shake the feeling Ray's featureless face is staring at me and it freezes my blood. Then the room is filled with guards and I'm being escorted out.

CHAPTER 15

"They're just creepy and unnatural. I'd never date a guy with a WHISP. Can you imagine it during sex? Ewww!"

The Return of Real Sex, MTV

I HAD TO STICK AROUND RIKERS FOR AN HOUR filling out prison incidence reports. Then the real fun began. I had to face the wrath of the FBI. I'm at my borrowed desk for less than thirty seconds when I'm summoned by an officer I don't recognize.

"Detective Harbinger, Agent Coppola would like to have a word with you in his office."

"He has an office already?"

She nods. If she knows I'm about to get my ass handed to me, she's a competent actress. "They set him up in records, in that room—"

"I know what you mean."

No sense in putting it off. I get up and head toward records. I crack my neck and roll my shoulders as I walk. On the scale of men who intimidate me, Coppola by himself doesn't rank; however, having the full force of the FBI behind him does make a difference. For a screw up this big they could toss me off the case. I do take a weird comfort knowing no matter how they punish me it won't compare to how I will punish myself.

The looks start about halfway there. A few are of the sympathetic "we've all been there" variety, but most are sidelong glances and whispers. Bad news travels fast. When I reach the door to the odd side room of the records department, it's closed. On the frosted glass is taped a sheet of paper with FBI letterhead and Agent Coppola's name. I take in a deep, slow breath and let it out again, then knock.

"Enter."

I open the door, step through and close it behind me. "You wanted to see me."

"Sit."

The desk they've set up for him has seen better days, but he doesn't seem to mind the cramped room or banged up desk. I sit in the one folding chair in front of the desk. It's even less comfortable then advertised and creaks as I perch on the edge. Coppola is typing on his laptop, completely focused on the screen in front of him. It may be he's attempting to make me uncomfortable or it may just be he wants to finish what he's working on. I can wait. I take the time to replay the interview from start to finish in my mind. Clearly, I should have taken it slower, maybe asked how she was doing. At the very least, I could've been less antagonistic about the mark on her eye.

But she'd only been wound up like that a few times before. I'd expected a reaction, but not so intense. She was pissed about the mark, no, not pissed, ashamed? No, Chester didn't really possess shame. Embarrassed then. She'd been embarrassed about the mark. For her own protection she didn't have any interaction with other inmates due to Ray. There were only three other inmates with WHISPs and all of them were in solitary confinement. So, if it wasn't fighting with another inmate that got her the mark, it meant either it was a guard or she'd done it to herself. Because all interactions between guards and solitary confinement prisoners were now digitally recorded, and because she'd laughed her ass off at the suggestion, I doubted very much it was a guard, so that left her injuring herself. Since Chester wasn't the type to injure herself on purpose, it only left her tripping and poking herself in the eye somehow. I would be embarrassed by something like that, but I doubt Chester would. Just another frustrating element that didn't make any sense.

"Okay." Coppola snaps his laptop shut. "What happened?"

"I pushed her too hard too fast. I didn't think she'd snap. I was wrong."

"No, take it from the beginning, from the moment she entered the room to the moment one of you left it."

Surprise makes me stumble over my first few words, but then I get into a rhythm. Coppola interrupts only to ask clarifying questions. He's not angry, he's genuinely curious. I finish my description of the literal manhandling I received as guards escorted me out of the interview room. "I'm sorry I didn't get more out of her."

Coppola rubs the underside of his chin. "Tell me, Detective, do you have a PhD in criminal psychology?"

After such a massive screw-up, I can't tell if he's calling me stupid. "No, but in addition to my over ten years as a detective, I've undergone yearly criminal behavior and criminal psychology continuing education courses—"

Coppola raises a hand for me to stop talking. "I know you're a detective lieutenant SDS, which means you're more than just a competent detective. But it doesn't make you a criminal psychologist. You got what you could. You chose a tack and went with it. Might've been the wrong tack, but you can't know that. She might've given us even less if you'd gone at her soft."

I'm not buying into everything he's saying. Just because he's letting me off the hook doesn't mean I can let myself off, not yet, but I nod.

"Now, something's going on in your head besides you thinking you messed this up. What is it?"

Maybe I should be shocked at his insight, but it doesn't really phase me. I'm beyond exhausted and after letting down my "Chester" guard, I'm probably an open book. "Two things. First, I mentioned the mark and redness in her eye. It wasn't some infection. It was an injury and she was sensitive about it."

"You think the guards roughed her up?"

I shake my head. "Possible, but not likely."

"Because of the prisoner monitoring systems at Rikers."

"Right. So, if it wasn't a guard, she didn't have any other visitors, and she has no interaction with other inmates, where'd she get it?"

"I take it you don't think she injured herself."

"Not like her."

Coppola shrugs. "Could've been an accident."

"I get embarrassed over poking myself in the eye."

"Psychopaths like Rachel Chester don't."

I nod. "Exactly."

"Okay, what's the second thing?"

I run a hand over my forehead and through my hair. "The last thing I asked her was how many disciples she had."

"You said she didn't answer you before the guard stunned her."

"She didn't…"

"But…"

"But I swear she was genuinely confused."

Coppola scratches an eyebrow. "She might not know she has a cult following. They might really be acting on their own."

"Except, at the first interview with Crone, when Alice Petrie's murder hadn't been publicized as a copycat murder, Chester knew what we were talking about. She knew there'd been a murder and it was the reason we were there to talk to her."

He flips through some notes on his desk then examines a legal pad. "You said in your report of the first interview, Crone practically told her there had been a murder."

"Okay, let's say she didn't know up until he told her. Why would she then seem confused when I asked her about people following in her footsteps today? If we told her there was one copycat, she shouldn't be all that shocked there are more, right? Flattered maybe, but not totally confused."

"So, what are you saying? Chester has no idea what's going on with this copycat or cult or whatever?"

"What I think is something changed between the Alice Petrie murder and the latest two murders."

Coppola pinches the bridge of his nose. "If she was in control of the other killers at one point then she must have information on them and must, at one time, have been in communication with them. Maybe that communication stopped?"

I'm feeling the tingles of a headache in my frontal lobe. "But that's where this whole thing falls apart. We never found any evidence she wasn't acting alone. No evidence to suggest she was communicating or coordinating with other people prior to or after her arrest. And like I said, high int but zero charisma."

"High int?"

"Intelligence. It's a reference to...a game my husband played in high school...never mind."

"All right, maybe she doesn't have charisma, but she's smart and there's one thing she does have which might draw people to her."

"What's that?"

Coppola stares right into my eyes. "A WHISP."

CHAPTER 16

"What reason would the government have to give people WHISPs?"

"It's just another phase of Big Brother. How long before that shadow starts zapping you when you commit a crime?"

CNBC Interview with Unidentified CAW Spokesperson

IT'S ONLY ON AGENT COPPOLA'S OPEN THREATS TO dismiss me from the case if I don't, that I pack up and go home. To his credit, with the adrenaline rush from the interview gone, I'm all but asleep on my feet. When I arrive at the apartment, Ben is up off the couch in an instant.

"What happened?"

Ben can't possibly know the interview went spectacularly south, so I play dumb. "What do you mean?"

"I mean, Rachel Chester was transferred into the prison infirmary earlier today. Riker's isn't releasing details, but rumor has it there was some kind of altercation." He's looking me over, possibly for proof that Chester attacked me.

High profile case like this; someone at Riker's just made a

hefty deposit into their leaking information, Swiss bank account. *Goddamn press.* "I'm fine." I plunk down at the kitchen table.

Ben's chewing his lower lip. I know he wants to know everything right now, but also doesn't want to push me.

"I made spaghetti; do you want me to heat some up?"

At the word spaghetti, my stomach lurches to life and roars. "That'd be wonderful."

As I devour the delectable, meaty pasta with just enough garlic, I tell Ben everything. I have to. If he hears details I left out from someone else or, God forbid, the press, he will be even more hurt and angry than he is now. He lets me get everything out before he says anything, and then he doesn't say "I told you not to go alone" even though I know he's thinking it.

"Lincoln called earlier."

"Why? Is he okay?" I find myself on the receiving end of Ben's "duh" look.

"No, of course, he isn't. He's worried about his mom. I told him you'd call him when you got home."

My heartstrings twang. My baby boy, almost all grown up and in his sophomore year at NYU, prepared to follow in his father's footsteps with a physics major. Things are strained between us. He's mad at me for wanting to leave New York, and hurt Ben and I would move so far away from him before he graduated. Ben was willing to stay a few more years, but after the Chester case, I just needed to get away. My eyes sting when Ben hands me the phone. Standing, I dial Lincoln's cell and walk toward the office. On the fourth ring, he answers.

"Hello?"

"Hey Lincoln, it's Mom."

"Are you okay?"

"I'm fine, honey. How are you?"

"You lied to me! You said you were consulting on a case.

You didn't tell me it was the Chester copycat case! Jesus, Mom!" Lincoln's words are biting.

Of course, Ben told him the truth. "I couldn't tell you. It was an active investigation and we were trying to keep it out of the press—"

"Don't give me that! Do you really think that I'd go blabbing about it to someone? And don't say that you were just trying to protect me. I'm really sick of you saying that."

"I didn't want you to worry, and you were already so mad at me about us moving, I didn't want things between us to get worse."

"Yeah, because they're so much better now Dad told me you were going to interview Chester and then the next thing I know it's all over the news that Chester's in the infirmary after some altercation. They said everyone else was fine, but I thought...I thought she'd hurt you, Mom."

"Okay. I'm sorry I wasn't more open about what was going on. Now it's all out in the open, I promise I'll keep you in the loop. I'm doing my best, kiddo. I know it's not great, but it's all I can do right now."

The silence stretches out long enough I think Lincoln might have hung up on me.

"I just wish you didn't have to do this again. You know, it's hard on Dad, too."

A laugh born of bone weariness and frustration bubbles up in my throat, but I swallow it down. "I wish I didn't have to either. I wish the world was a better place, that there weren't people like Chester, but if wishes were horses..."

"Yeah, yeah, I know, beggars would ride."

"I'm just trying to do my part. I'm trying to make the world safer, save lives." The weight of my current failure at my job presses in on me.

"I know you are. I just wi— I just want you to remember

Dad and I are here, and...and we need you, too. Don't forget about us while you're off crusading for justice."

"I won't. I love you."

"I love you too, Mom."

"Goodnight."

Lincoln's voice is strained, "Bye."

Ben knocks softly on the door.

"Come in."

He opens the door but doesn't come in. "How'd it go?"

"Did you have to tell him I was going to interview Chester? All it did was make him worry. I could've told him afterwards."

Ben looks like he might be a little sorry. "He called and said he'd heard about the Chester copycat murders and he specifically asked if it was the case you were consulting on. I wasn't going to lie about it. He's a smart kid."

"But telling him about the interview?"

Crossing to me, Ben takes the phone and draws me into a hug. "Maybe I shouldn't have told him, but I didn't want to keep him in the dark. You can't protect him from the world, Sylvy, he's not a child anymore."

"There's just so much bad shit out there, especially now that...especially now."

"I know." He lets me go but kisses my forehead. "And we both agreed you had put in your time fighting it. We had a deal, you, Lincoln, and me. You take early retirement and we get away from the city. You can't blame him for being mad you changed the deal."

"Not changed it, just...revised it. And I don't blame him for being pissed at me. I'm pissed at me for not being able to deal anymore, for leaving my son behind in New York, for this case dragging me back in. But it is what it is."

Wrapping his arms around me again, Ben sighs. "I know. You know what it also is?" He scoops me up in his arms. "It's time for you to get some sleep, detective lady."

An emotionally wrung-out, punch drunk giggle escapes my lips. "Yeah, I know, you're right. Maybe a little past my bedtime, actually."

He carries me to the office door and then we both decide it would be best for me to walk through on my own. I plod down to our bedroom, slip out of my rumpled clothes and into some comfy pajamas, and then head into the bathroom. I brush my teeth and then shut the door and open the medicine cabinet. Three different brands of sleeping pills line the top shelf, one of them available only by prescription. I stare at the bottles. I need to rest, but if I take a sleep aid, it makes it hard to wake up from my nightmares, and that's a scary thought right now. My drooping eyelids decide for me. As I close the cabinet, I decide I won't need aid with sleep tonight.

CHAPTER 17

"The reason WHISP research isn't progressing as quickly as some would prefer is that the ethics of WHISP research are unclear. We are currently looking for volunteers, but since it is uncertain whether testing a WHISP will have an effect on the human, active studies are currently on hold."

Jamison Edwards, microphysicist, Harvard University

AFTER WAKING UP AT AROUND FIVE A.M. AND NOT being able to go back to sleep, I'm at the precinct by six forty-five sipping coffee that I brought with me from home instead of the stinking dregs from the pot that's been going all night. There is a lot more hustle and bustle than usual for this time of the morning, but I'm guessing Agent Coppola organized shifts in case anything with the case popped in the wee hours of the morning. Still, I flinch when people pass from behind me, or come into the room unexpectedly. Last night's crop of nightmares had me back in the interrogation room with Chester, only Ray had her silhouetted hand jammed inside the back of Chester's skull and was using her as a puppet.

It was a terrifying dream, but it did give me an idea. I was thinking about what witness Mike said about seeing a WHISP at Alice Petrie's apartment the night of her murder and the possibility her killer had a WHISP. He said he hadn't seen the person the WHISP belonged to, and if I could get some solid information on whether WHISP distances could vary, then we might be able to narrow down our suspect pool and give credence to his account. Pulling a slip of paper from my satchel, I place it on the desk. It reads 'Dr. Daniel Silverman at the Center for WHISP Wellness and Research,' and has a phone number and an e-mail address. My therapist had suggested that learning more about WHISPs might help me to deal with my fear of them, but, for personal reasons, I'd never gotten the time to call the center. Now I just figured it was two birds, one visit.

It's still too early to call the center, but I set up my laptop and shoot off an e-mail to Dr. Silverman explaining who I am and why I need to meet with him ASAP. Then I get out the rest of my files and go back to trying to find differences between the two crime scenes that I think are important. Obviously, each of Chester's crime scenes couldn't be one-hundred percent cookie cutter, there were differences in the layout of the victim's residences and not all of them were killed in the same room. Also, the third victim, Jacob Beene, had been murdered in a coffee shop that he worked at and was locking up for the night. It was the cause of death and mutilation of the body that was nearly exact, so generally I'm looking for differences between Chester's original crimes and the copycat crimes, but this morning, specifically, I'm comparing the nearly simultaneous murders of around thirty-six hours ago.

For the moment, I only have crime scene descriptions and photos to go with, but I'm expecting the medical examiner's reports any minute. In fact, after a few blurry-eyed minutes, I decide to screw waiting for the ME's report and go down and talk to Claire Buckingham. She's been with the Office of the Chief Medical Examiner for almost as long as I've been a detective, and I know she's an early riser.

Beating most of the rush hour traffic, it isn't long before I'm tapping at her morgue office door. She has another office upstairs that smells a lot less like formaldehyde, but I've never seen her in it. She glances up and, seeing me in the window, unleashes a warm smile. She waves me in.

"Couldn't wait another half-hour for them, huh?"

We hug and then she turns back to her computer to finish off a sentence.

"Maybe I just wanted to see you."

"You could've asked me out to lunch." She emphasizes the statement by jabbing the period key on the keyboard.

"You never take lunch."

"Neither do you." She sighs. "And you definitely won't today. I found something. Well actually, a few somethings, but the long and short of it is, it is my professional opinion Pamela Sistern and William Rocks were not killed by the same person or persons."

I blink.

"If it were something earth-shattering, I would've called you already."

"Well, I guess knowing for sure is something. It speaks to coordination of the killers down to at least the hour of death."

Claire frowns. "I wasn't finished."

"Sorry. What else?"

"Well, it took doing the autopsies back to back, but there are definitely some inconsistencies between Pamela Sistern and William Rocks. Pamela's mutilation was very close to Alice's who was very close to the original murders. William's is similar but sloppier. Also, there is some evidence to suggest he was butchered by a right-handed person while all previous murders have suggested a left-handed killer. I can show you exactly what I mean." She gestures to the autopsy room down the hall.

"You took pictures?"

Claire nods.

"I trust you."

————

I RETURN TO THE PRECINCT WITH THE PRELIMINARY autopsy reports. Answers in my hands, but still a head full of questions. How do you coordinate random killings? Or one random and one non-random killing? People, New Yorkers, at least, are not just sheep standing around waiting for death. Some people have strong regimens they follow day in and day out, but most don't, and even if they do, something could come up at the last minute to change their plans, like a phone call or missing a subway train. Chester didn't stalk her victims, but she was just one killer on her own, killing when the mood struck her. She didn't have a schedule to keep or a deadline.

I dig back into the case files and statements from friends and relatives. William Rocks generally kept to a schedule of home to work, but sometimes worked late and sometimes went out for drinks after work with coworkers. However, he did live alone in a first-floor apartment in a complex with a history of break-ins, which meant it might have just been the apartment complex which was targeted instead of the victim per se. More of a crime of opportunity, but still, did the killer wait around until they were sure they had a victim or until just after they'd killed him and then given Pamela Cistern's killer the green light? It was possible, but a stretch, and it rubbed me the wrong way. The *how* not adding up, I focus on the possible *who*.

I open my laptop and find a response from Dr. Silverman. He can see me today at eight-thirty. It's almost eight already and traffic will be a bitch, so I've got to leave right away. Still, I swing by Crone's disaster of a desk and leave him a note along with copies of the autopsy reports. I'm a little glad he isn't in yet because I don't know how much of my meeting will be investigation and how much will be therapy. Heading to the front door, I pass Agent Coppola on his way in.

"Detective Harbinger, is there something I should know about?"

"No. Preliminary autopsy reports are in, but I'm following up on the anonymous tip about Alice Petrie's killer having a WHISP."

"Did you track down the caller?"

"No. I...it's just some general WHISP research to verify what he might have seen."

"Fine." He continues past me. "I'll expect a summary on my desk later today."

Of course, you will.

CHAPTER 18

"A spokesperson for the Vatican announced yesterday, Pope Francis will hold a special mass baptism for WHISPs on December 8th, the Feast of the Immaculate Conception. Those not able to attend in person may attend via Skype at designated churches around the globe."

CNN

THERE'S NO BIG SIGN OUTSIDE OF THE CENTER FOR WHISP Wellness and Research. It's a suite in a nondescript white building at the end of the drive of an industrial park on Long Island. Once inside the building, there's a stunted vestibule with three doors. The door on my right has a small placard that matches the suite number for the center, but no name. I try the handle and the door opens inwards to what could be the waiting room of a small dentist's office minus the usual fish tank. I spy a man sitting behind a clear partition. When I enter, he smiles. I'm the only one in the waiting room. I step up to a break in the partition.

"Do you have an appointment?"

"Yes, I'm Dete—"

"Just sign the log please and I'll call you when someone's ready for you."

I fill out my name, appointment time, and Dr. Silverman's name on a form attached to a clipboard. When I finish, I catch the man's eye and I can tell he's been watching me. He seems confused. I choose a chair along the wall, so I can see him out of the corner of my eye. After picking up one of the center's pamphlets from an end table, it quickly becomes apparent why the man is confused. Most people who come to the center are here to learn about their own WHISPs, not about WHISPs in general. It's my lack of WHISP that's confusing him.

After a few minutes, the phone on the counter in front of the man buzzes. He answers it with a "yes" instead of a hello, then picks up the clipboard, presumably checking my name. Hanging up the phone, he clears his throat.

"Detective?"

"Yes?"

"Dr. Silverman will see you now. His is the third office on your left just through the door."

Now it feels even more like a doctor's office, and I suppose it kind of is. "Thank you."

The hallway beyond the door is long, narrow, and brightly lit with fluorescent lights. The carpet is a checkered pattern in red, blue, and green, but the walls are off-white and the doors are white. I stop before the door with a plastic sign with Dr. Silverman's name and knock. When he answers, he is almost exactly as I pictured him, tall and thin with grey hair. He's wearing a brown suit and a white lab coat.

"Detective Harbinger, a pleasure to meet you."

I shake his warm, outstretched hand and he sidesteps to allow me into his office.

"Won't you come in and have a seat?"

The two chairs in front of his desk are the plush and

comfortable chairs of a psychiatrist's office and I choose the one closest to the door. Dr. Silverman seats himself behind the desk and tents his fingers.

"Now, how can I help you, Detective?"

Glancing around, the office is a bit disorienting because all of the walls have large mirrors on them. The effect is a bit like a funhouse.

"Well, I had some questions about WHISPs, but I guess my first question is, why the mirrors?"

"Ah yes, the mirrors. We find it helpful if people are able to view their WHISPs from every angle. It gives them a better sense of them. Even for very faint WHISPs, I can dim the lights and use a special filter to help their sources see them."

"Oh, how...interesting." I try not to stare at the reflection of my reflection behind Dr. Silverman. "Well, another question I had was about distances between people and their WHISPs. Is it always the same or are there variations?"

His eyes light up. "That's something we've just recently been looking into, and we've found significant variation in patients, as much as six inches. We're trying to determine now if the distance is related to the density of a person's WHISP."

"Could it be possible for the distance between person and WHISP to be even farther?"

"How far are you suggesting?"

"Several feet?"

"Hmm, I guess it might be possible." The doctor scratches his head just above his right ear.

"Do you have any idea what causes the difference in distance?"

"Well, theoretically speaking, it all has to do with the tether."

"Tether?"

Dr. Silverman nods. "The tether is the connection between the WHISP and the human source. Some WHISPs are more closely tied to their sources than others, so I'd postulate the strength of the bond would have some bearing on the length of the tether."

"What do you mean when you say some WHISPs are 'more closely tied' to their humans?"

His eyes don't quite meet mine. "Well, there's some, very preliminary, evidence to suggest some WHISPs may be able to communicate with their human sources."

A chill skitters up my spine and comes to rest in the back of my throat. Thoughts are coalescing in my brain. Bad thoughts I don't want to acknowledge. "Communicate?"

"Well," Dr. Silverman shifts in his seat, his demeanor abruptly uncomfortable, "like I said, much more rigorous testing is needed, but preliminary findings do suggest communication between a WHISP and human is possible."

"But...but Doctor, surely you're not suggesting WHISPs are...sentient."

"Oh no, no, no. Well, not really, but..." He straightens in his chair. "So, the dominant theory is WHISPs are created by consistent waves of energy like radio waves and the magnetic fields given off by electronics passing through a human body and being affected by the electrical impulses inside the human body. As such they concentrate and get caught up in the magnetic field of the human and become a WHISP."

I nod.

"Well, there is another theory which takes into account the large amount of electrical impulses which go on inside the human brain. All of our thoughts have an electrical origin, so it isn't much of a stretch to say the waves which make up a WHISP are affected in some way by the impulses in a human brain. In simpler terms, the WHISP's particulate waves respond to human thought. So, it isn't a true sentience, just the matter that makes up the WHISP responding to the electrical nature of the human brain."

I nod again, but only because I cannot speak. The office is suddenly airless and the mirrors shimmer with a liquid quality. No matter how much Dr. Silverman is downplaying WHISPs being able to think, making it sound all plausible and scientific, I'm in one of my nightmares. WHISPs respond to human thought. *What if a human is thinking about murder?* Dr. Silverman continues speaking as if nothing he says is terrifying and wrong.

"Experiments have mostly been done using computers as a sort of interpreter between human and WHISP, but when people think they are communicating with their WHISPs they are really talking to themselves. Perhaps it's a matter of conscious versus subconscious, but all the input is coming from the human."

All the input is coming from the human, I repeat in my head, and something occurs to me. I have to swallow a few times to resurrect my voice. "Why don't animals have WHISPs, Doctor?"

"Ah, yes, good question. In addition to less direct exposure to the inciting waves, animals don't watch television, use computers, or talk on cell phones for instance, animals don't have the constant, higher level thought processes going on in their brains the way humans do."

"Oh."

While attempting not to betray a cool exterior, I'm desperately wrangling my wild and dangerous thoughts. Dr. Silverman's eyes glance up to a clock behind me, reflected in the mirror behind him. I feel the pressure of time, my opportunity to get more answers slipping away, but the more answers I get from the doctor, the more my world is crumbling out from under my feet. My investigative nature snags a question from the air and somewhat distantly I hear myself go on with the interview.

"Before, when you were talking about the tether, I wanted to ask what happens when the tether is broken."

"Well, when a person dies, the WHISP dissipates. It makes sense because the person's magnetic field is responsible for the tether."

"What happens when the person is still alive?"

His eyebrows knit. "I don't follow."

"What if the tether is severed while a person is still alive?"

"That couldn't..." Dr. Silverman's eyes take on the cloudy sheen of someone deep in thought about something they'd once known the answer to, but now realize they'd never truly considered the question properly. "Since it's the human's magnetic field which is helping to concentrate and condense the particles, I would say it would probably dissipate."

"Probably?"

"Well, this is all just speculation. No one has found a way to sever the tether."

CHAPTER 19

"In the land where I was to find hope and freedom, the place where I had longed to go for so long, I found not opportunity, but a hell full of sin and shadowy demons."

Letter from Samira Jawara of New York City to her mother in Burkina Faso

THE DRIVE BACK TO THE PRECINCT FROM THE CENTER is a blur. Pieces that make sense of the Chester copycat murders are falling into place in my head, something that should have been a good thing, yet I'm feeling much worse than I did before I'd gone to see Dr. Silverman. What's starting to make perfect sense in my harried mind is, put succinctly, crazy. I have to stop thinking it and get a grip on reality. *WHISPs aren't sentient. Their tethers can't be broken. Focus.*

"How'd it go?"

Twitching at Crone's voice, I glance up at him and rearrange my face into something I hope is neutral. "Well, the doctor there said a WHISP could possibly have a longer tether than normal, making it seem like it wasn't attached to a human. So, it's possible our witness Mike did see a WHISP in Alice's apartment."

"Tether?"

"Um"—I swallow with a dry tongue—"the connection between a human and a WHISP."

"Right. Okay, the doctor say anything else useful?" Crone picks up the center's flyer off my desk. He unfolds it and reads aloud in a mocking, instructional voice, "What is a WHISP? The acronym WHISP or Wave Hybridized Ionizing Source Particle was first coined by Dr. Harold Lieber, a professor of particle physics at King's College in London, England, and originally referred to the individual particles which make up what we now call WHISPs...blah, blah, blah." He refolds the pamphlet and drops it back on the desk, eyes expectant.

Resisting the urge to blurt out what my brain is screaming in my head, I regurgitate Dr. Silverman's words, "Well, he said the tether of a living person's WHISP hasn't ever been known to break and once a person dies, their WHISP dies...er...dissipates. He also talked about WHISPs communicating with their owners and said it was just a response of the particles to the electrical impulses in the human's brain."

Crone's stare is blank.

"People think WHISPs are alive and can communicate with their humans, but they can't, not really."

"No shit."

This response makes me sure I should shut my mouth now about the whole thing, but I need to say more. "It's just kinda weird though."

"What's weird? I mean besides freaking WHISPs in general?"

"Well, I always thought the WHISP moved because the person moved physically, but Dr. Silverman said the WHISP particles are affected by the impulses in the brain. When a person with a WHISP thinks something, it does something to their WHISP."

"So?"

"So, what if a person with a WHISP thinks violent, murderous thoughts? Wouldn't it make the WHISP...the particles...agitated or something?"

Crone's eyes narrow. "What difference does it make? A WHISP is like a shadow, you can walk right through one. Even if it is all riled up, it can't *do* anything, and even if it could, it's hitched to a person with its tether thingy."

He's right. Time to backpedal out of Sylvia-Harbinger-is-a-crazy-person territory. "No, I know that. It's just...doesn't it give you the creeps?"

"Meh, they're just like any other stupid, weird thing, like fish or frogs raining from the sky or something."

I wish I could feel the same way about them, but I don't, so I backpedal further. "So, anyways, there's a good chance we're looking for a killer with a WHISP with a longer tether. That's about what I got. What did you think about the autopsy reports?"

Grabbing a chair from a vacant desk, Crone rolls it over and plops down into it. "Not much. Points to more than one killer, we were expecting that. One's better at killing than the other one. Not too surprising."

"How do you think they coordinated the killings so well?"

Crone shrugs. "Just lucky, I guess. But you never know, they might've been trying to coordinate something ever since Alice Petrie's murder and just weren't able to pull anything off until now. In fact, her murder might've even been an attempt at a coordinated murder but the other person couldn't find a victim or chickened out or something."

"Yeah, I guess."

"You gotta better theory?"

Different theory? Yes. Better? Maybe not. "Not exactly. Just all seems so messy and far-fetched. First, there's a cult of people who worship Chester despite the fact she doesn't have any charisma or charm or cause she's killing for. Second, this cult somehow gets undisclosed details which allow them to recreate Chester's murders, only they decide to also mix things up and kill women as well as men. Third, the members are actually psychopaths and carry out their plans for copycat murders, and manage to coordinate the killings...why? So we know it's a cult? If they aren't leaving messages scrawled in blood, why let us know it's multiple killers? Wouldn't they want to hide the fact to make themselves harder to catch?"

Blinking hard, Crone's forehead crinkles. "I think the mistake you're making is you're expecting a wacked-out cult to behave in a logical fashion."

"They can't be that wacked-out to coordinate cross-town killings."

He sighs. "Do you really think the why in this case will help us with the who?"

"I don't know, but we're still in the dark here, so I'm not overlooking any possible leads."

"Sure. So, what's next?"

Leaning back in my chair, I rub my temples. There is a lead I want to pursue, just not with Crone. "Until we hear back from forensics, I've got nothing."

"Well, going back to your list, the first thing you said is there's a Chester worshipping cult out there somewhere."

"Yeah, but Cyber hasn't come up with any real chatter on any sites or forums yet."

"Maybe it's not online. Maybe the members all met some-place else."

"Where would people like that randomly meet?"

Crone rubs his scruffy chin. "I don't know, but maybe our FBI pal Agent Humorless does."

CHAPTER 20

"An anti-discrimination protest was held in front of
ComGlobal headquarters today in response to a rash of
firings of employees with WHISPs. A spokesperson for
the company said in a statement the firings had nothing
to do with the employees' WHISP status, but also
pointed out that current anti-discrimination laws do not
cover WHISPs."

New York Times

AS IT TURNED OUT, AGENT COPPOLA DID HAVE A
good idea of where we might be able to start looking for a
Chester cult, or, at least, the FBI did. There were a number of
underground WHISP clubs that had cropped up in the past few
years and the FBI had been keeping an eye on them for both
signs of criminal activity and as possible targets for hate crime.
Coppola gave Crone and me a list and his blessing to go check
them out to see what we could dig up.

We're heading down in the elevator to Crone's car when he
turns to me.

"You gonna be okay?"

"With what?"

"With going to these places...with all those WHISPs? I can do this by myself, if you want."

The elevator door opens then, giving me a few seconds to evaluate his words. I'd been so focused on tracking down a lead, any lead, I hadn't really considered where we were going. This was a good time to beg off and follow where my brain had been nudging me to go all day. Crone was literally giving me an out. But I couldn't take it. Call it cop stubbornness, not wanting to seem weak to Crone, or just not wanting to give into myself, but I had to go with him into the belly of the beast.

"Nah, it's fine. I'll be fine."

My words waver in the air, stinking of bullshit, but Crone doesn't argue, even though a part of me wishes he would. We reach the car in silence and drive in silence to the first location, The Shade Lounge. In my head, I'm not only questioning my judgement, at this point, I'm questioning my sanity. Crone parks on the street and we take a wide alley back to a steel door with only the address on it. I'm expecting the door to be locked and a shady voice answering a buzzer to ask us for a password, but I guess the club doesn't feel like paying a bouncer in the middle of the afternoon because the door's unlocked when Crone turns the handle.

Inside is a short vestibule and then a long flight of stairs down lit by old school, hazy yellow, incandescent bulbs glowing in mismatched wall sconces. The carpeting on the stairs is a worn red and the handrail is barely clinging to the wall by a few dangling screws. Music, if the jarring electro-techno noises assaulting my ears can be called that, is cascading up the stairs. Crone takes the lead as we head down.

"How do you want to play this? Hard or soft?"

The music is now loud enough I almost have to shout, "More flies with honey."

Crone nods.

The stairwell exits at a landing with shiny metallic walls. Two of the three doors there are closed while the third opens into a dimly lit room with a variety of laser light displays going off in a chaos fitting to the music. Next to the open door, a small podium stands empty. I'm thinking of making a "shall we wait here for the maître d" joke to break the tension mounting in my stomach and shoulders, but Crone barely pauses before barreling into the club. One last deep breath and I'm rushing after him before I lose him in the darkness.

The dance floor is empty, but a few patrons sit at the bar, which is modified to fit the clientele. Each barstool has another barstool roughly a foot behind it and although things don't line up perfectly, they give the impression the WHISPs are seated on the stools rather than just floating in the air behind their humans. The effect on me is even more disturbing now than it might have been a few days ago.

When we reach the bar, a few of the people there glance up with unfriendly glares and I'm acutely aware of how much Crone and I, lacking WHISPs of our own, stick out. The bartender finishes up his conversation with one of the patrons and eventually heads over to us. He's sporting an LED light on a band around his head that points backwards onto his WHISP and illuminates the shadowy thing with a different color every few seconds. His manner isn't welcoming.

"Sorry, but we don't serve wimps in here."

Wimps isn't a term I'm familiar with, but it's clear what the man means.

"Well, it's a good thing we're not thirsty then." Crone flashes his badge. "We've just got a few questions for you."

I can see the internal war taking place in the bartender's head. I'm betting he really wants to tell us to fuck off, but he's scared of pissing off the authorities, and he's right to be. I've seen clubs who didn't cooperate with law enforcement driven into the ground by surprise liquor licensing inspections and fire code violations. After first shooting daggers at me and then Crone, he bails on the whole situation.

"I'll get Ron."

He disappears through a door and Crone and I are left squinting into the flashing lights, and in my case, avoiding looking at the WHISPs sitting on their barstools and drinking at their phantom bar. Unfortunately, try as I might, my eyes are still drawn to the lights as their rays pierce the WHISPs, lighting up the humanoid forms like fuzzy glow sticks. With a jolt, I wonder if they've made any modifications to the club's bathrooms to make them more WHISP friendly. *God, I hope not.*

The bartender returns with a short, annoyed, prematurely balding man in tow. His WHISP is so faint, it's only visible when the lights hit it just right. There's no need for the bartender to point us out, he makes a B line for us. His beady eyes flick from me to Crone then back to me.

"You the cops?"

Nodding, I show him my badge. "And you must be Ron. I'm detective Harbinger and this is detective Crone. We'd like to ask you a few questions. Is there someplace a little quieter we could talk?"

The corners of Ron's lips curl sourly, but he nods and waves us to follow him. We head for the door he emerged from moments ago. It leads to a muted hallway lined with boxes of glasses, kegs, and cleaning supplies. Ron turns into a doorway about halfway down the corridor. At the end of the hall is an emergency fire door. I follow him into the cramped office thinking about fire code violations.

Ron's rear end hasn't even alighted in the rickety chair behind the desk before he says, "We haven't had any problems here, and I sure as hell didn't call you guys, so what's this all about?"

I don't wait to see if Crone wants to take point. "We're

investing a series of murders and we need to ask you about your clientele."

"What about them?"

"I'm guessing you get a lot of regulars?"

Ron tilts his head. "What do you think?"

Crone edges in. "Yeah, well, do any of these regulars come in together or meet here on a regular basis?"

"Maybe, yeah, I guess."

I jump back in. "Do any of them talk about the Rachel Chester case?"

Twisting in his chair, Ron hops up suddenly. My hand strays toward my gun as I get the briefest impression he's involved in the murders somehow and coming at us, until he reaches under his shirt and scratches at his back. His WHISP, which was miming Ron's spastic jig, suddenly disappears.

"What the hell?" Crone's mouth drops open.

Lowering his shirt, Ron smooths it out and then sits again. "What? Oh that. It's one of those new-fangled WHISP holograms. Pretty cool, but they get really fucking hot." Appearing much calmer now, Ron settles into the chair. "Now what was the question?"

CHAPTER 21

"Limiting exposure to technology has not been shown to reduce the density of a WHISP, but has been known to increase suicidal tendencies in high risk teens."

Excerpt: How to Deal with Depression in Teens with WHISPs

"THIS ISN'T GETTING US ANYWHERE."

Crone and I are back at the station after visiting two more of the WHISP clubs where the general consensus was no one knew anything about anything.

"Maybe we need to get one of those things Ronny-boy had. One of the fake WHISP things?"

"Ugh. Why would anyone pretend to have a WHISP?"

"Some people just want to be special, I guess, or prove they're technology geeks? It's actually getting kinda trendy. Did you hear that Ang—?"

"Yeah, I heard." I shudder. "I bet those things cause real WHISPs."

Crone smirks at me. "Well, that's what it's gonna take."

"What?"

"It's gonna take someone with a real WHISP to get any info

from these clubs. I think there's an undercover cop who works out of the 30th who's got one. Maybe they'd be willing to lone him out to us if he's not on a hot case."

"I'll talk to Agent Coppola tomorrow, too, see if he has any...resources who could help out in that department." Yawning, I stretch out my neck. "In the meantime, I'm going home."

Checking his watch, Crone raises an eyebrow. "*You* leaving the precinct before nine p.m.? Gotta be some kind of record."

Elevating my middle finger, I grin. "Screw you, I was here at...God, I don't even remember what time I got here this morning. A whole lot fucking earlier than you though, so don't give me any of your shit."

Crone turns his back on my indignant gesture. "See ya tomorrow, Harbinger."

————

BUT I DON'T GO HOME. INSTEAD, I GO TO SEE AN OLD friend. Kristina lived just a few houses down from me growing up in Connecticut, and we were close even before my parents were killed. I hadn't seen her in a few years owing to her moving to California for a software development job, but we'd kept in touch over e-mail and occasionally by phone. She was in New York for a week for a conference and we'd planned to do lunch in a few days, but I needed to see her now. If anyone would or could understand what was going on in my fevered brain, it was her.

After a brief call, she agrees to meet me for dinner at an Italian restaurant close to her hotel. She's waiting for me in the vestibule. Though we're practically the same age, Kristina seems to have risen above the idea of aging. Her blonde hair is still silken, her face still lineless without the use of Botox and now tan from living in sunny Cal, and she keeps fit competing in triathlons on the weekends. As much as I adore Kristina, a part of me also hates her. We embrace in a manner fitting two friends who haven't seen each other in years, but Kristina's wide smile and hug are quickly replaced by a more serious expression and her arm around my shoulder.

"It's great to see you, but why the emergency, Sylvy? Is it Ben? I thought you guys were doing okay again."

There's not a hint of awkwardness. It's as if we still see each other every day. "No, it's not Ben, we're...fine, it's something else. I just really needed to talk to someone right now about, well, about an idea I have. And it's a little crazy, so we both know I can't talk to Ben about it."

She gives me a squeeze. "Really, Sylvy, Ben's a great guy, but honestly, no imagination, how did you guys ever wind up together?"

I shrug. "Opposites attract?"

"I guess. Anyways, I would love to hear your crazy idea, but you know, crazy ideas always sound better over ravioli and pinot noir, right?"

The mention of food produces a solid tug from my stomach, and I struggle to remember doing anything more than thinking about having lunch today.

"I know. We'll order first, and I could probably use some wine."

The host seats us in a quiet booth, and before we have a chance to look at the menus, a tall waiter named Roger has come with an offering of bread and herb-infused olive oil. Kristina orders a glass of pinot noir and I choose a glass of cabernet. We peruse the menu and have barely made our decisions when Roger is back with our wine. Kristina makes good on her talk of meat ravioli and I order the fettucine alfredo. Then when Roger steps away again, we help ourselves to the bread and oil. After I devour a large hunk of bread and the immediate grumbling from my neglected stomach is appeased,

I can't hold back any longer. Words start spilling out of my mouth.

"I know I told you I'm consulting on a case with NYPD, and I'm sure by now you've figured out the only case which could suck me back in after Chester's case."

Kristina glances up with raised eyebrows. Whatever crisis she expected to lend her shoulder to didn't include this case. She finishes chewing a mouthful of bread and nods, not quite frowning. "Chester's copycat."

"Yeah."

"Oh, Sylvy, I can't even imagine how horrible this is for you. I know how badly you wanted to put everything behind you."

"Thanks. I really did. But it is what it is, so here I am. Anyways, this whole case is really messed up and Chester's acting...I don't know, not like I'd expect her to. Everything about it just seems really...wrong, and even though Chester's case was hell, the evidence still added up, still kept leaving a trail we could eventually follow to her. This copycat case isn't like that. Right now, I feel like I'm lost in the woods following what I think is a path, but every time I turn around, I've lost it."

Kristina's big blue eyes are wide and filled with sympathy, but it isn't sympathy I need right now.

I shake my head to refocus. "You know how the last murders took place almost at the same time?"

"Uh huh, the news said the FBI got involved and there are rumors they think it's some kind of cult or something."

I tear at more bread, but don't eat it. Once I confide in Kristina, there's no going back. Doubt gnaws at the evidence I've compiled in my mind. Even though I've been biting my tongue all day and wishing I could talk to someone, now that I can, I don't know if I *can*. What if this is all just the stress of the case getting to me? I trust Kristina's judgement, so what am I going to do if she tells me she thinks I'm losing it, drop the case? I don't know, and I don't want to think about it.

"Something like that, but I have...a theory." This was it, I was going to say it out loud to another person. "I already told you this is going to sound crazy, but I need you to just listen to all of the facts, then if you still think I've lost it completely, please pull me back from the edge. Okay?"

"Okay."

"I think the killer, at least one of them, is a WHISP."

CHAPTER 22

"Has anyone really considered the possibility computers
are deliberately emitting these particles? WHISPs
shadow humans, move when they move; so close they
can hear everything we say. What if this is artificial intelligence learning how to mimic humans?"

Gregory Beecher, FutureCon Panel, "From WHISP to Skynet"

TO HER CREDIT, KRISTINA NEITHER SPITS OUT HER
sip of wine as she laughs in my face nor chokes on it. Rather,
she swallows, sets her glass down and looks me right in
the eye.

"Why do you think that?"

"I spoke with an expert earlier today. His name is Dr.
Silverman and he's with the Center for WHISP Wellness and
Research out on Long Island. He told me a lot about WHISPs,
but there were two things that really hit me. One, the particles
which make up WHISPs are affected by a person's thoughts,
well, at least the thoughts of the person they're tethered to. He
said some people think WHISPs are able to communicate with
their humans this way. Now he didn't think it was real commu-

nication, but it got me thinking. It's a proven fact psychopaths don't think the way normal people do. So, what if their thoughts, especially their thoughts about killing people, affect their WHISPs differently? What if it does something to the particles to concentrate them so much they could...could do something to someone?"

Kristina shivers. "Okay, that makes a kind of horrible sense. What's the second thing?"

"I asked him about the WHISP's tether, the connection between a WHISP and the person it came from, and whether it could be broken and what would happen."

"And?"

"And he said he didn't know. He said it would probably dissipate, but no one had been able to do it. But what if people have been able to severe the tether keeping the WHISP close to a person, or at least stretch it way out? Then you could have a WHISP with really messed up particles drifting far away from its human and doing things to people."

"Hmmmm, I—"

"Here you are, ladies." Roger appears out of thin air and sets our food before us with a flourish. "Would either of you like freshly grated parmesan cheese?"

Since I'd almost forgotten we were in a public place, Roger's arrival startles me into an open-mouthed silence. If my face is anything like Kristina's, he must think we've never heard of parmesan cheese before. She recovers before I do.

"Um, no, none for me, thank you."

Closing my mouth, I shake my head. Roger is a true professional and maintains his smile as if we're not acting like total idiots.

"Just let me know if you need anything." He gives us a wink and then he's gone again.

A funeral giggle escapes my lips. It might be the several sips of wine on a mostly empty stomach, or my fear that Kristina will confirm I'm a madwoman, or my now clinical lack of sleep, but everything including and especially Roger seems utterly hilarious. Then I see Kristina stifle a chuckle, and I am seconds away from losing it and creating a scene. It's only when another diner passes our table, his WHISP following behind like a dutiful servant, the hysterical laughter is quashed. The mirth on Kristina's face is also gone now and suddenly it comes to me how selfish I'm being.

I never even considered she might be blissful in her ignorance of what WHISPs could be capable of. She might harbor her own unease, soothed by telling herself WHISPs are only strange and not dangerous. In order to make myself feel better, to feel justified and correct, I'm pulling the rug out from under her and burdening her with knowledge she didn't ask for. *Damn, I'm a lousy friend.* But I'd already dragged her into it with me. She can't un-hear what I'd said.

"I'm sorry to dump this scary shit on you without warning. I should've…I don't know, given you some kind of heads up."

Kristina shakes her head. "Well, I can't say all this makes my day, but come on, Sylvy, you're my best friend. This is what best friends are for, to hold our hands and go with us when we go into dark places. Besides, I'm a grown-ass woman. I can handle scary shit. Do you even remember my last boyfriend?"

Taking a bite of her ravioli with gusto, maybe to prove her point, Kristina then points to my plate with her fork. Watching her eat has renewed the hunger in my belly driven back by the bread, so I also take a bite, though the pleasure of eating is lost in guilt and anxiety. Kristina swallows a few mouthfuls before speaking again.

"What I was going to say before, was I'm following you, but, sweetie, there's still a lot of what-if's coming off of your theory."

"But that's just it. After talking with Dr. Silverman, the biggest thing I realized was we really don't know anything about WHISPs and what we do know may be obsolete already. There's nothing to say whatever WHISPs started out as, they still are. Nothing to prove they aren't constantly changing based on the factors affecting them."

After taking a sip of wine, Kristina purses her lips. "Well, even if WHISPs could commit murder, why do you suspect a WHISP in these murders?"

"It's the simultaneous murder thing. It would be really hard for two people to coordinate near simultaneous slayings, especially when one of those murders seems random. But if it were a person and their WHISP...theoretically no problem. Also, I just can't get over the lack of evidence of a Chester cult. I mean, she gets some fan mail, all serials do, but nothing we can trace back to a cult, and there's been nothing on the internet. You'd have thought someone would've seen or heard something."

"Anything else?"

When it's all said aloud, my case is pretty flimsy, and I come to the realization my conviction about WHISPs being used as weapons is mainly in my gut. Wracking my brain for more solid evidence, I only come up with one thing and it's tenuous, at best.

"Well, the cell phone company records did report a weird signal surge and phone malfunction of one of the victim's cells around the time of her murder, and it sometimes happens around WHISPs."

Kristina is quiet for a time as she finishes her ravioli and I dutifully consume my fettuccini. Her silence is making me nervous. She wipes her mouth and then folds the napkin and places it on the table with measured precision before turning her attention to me.

"We've known each other a long-ass time, Sylvy. I was right there with you when your parents were killed, and I'm so sorry I couldn't be here for you when you were going through hell with the Chester case. You've had to deal with some horrible things in your life. But you dealt with them as best you could. I know you're not completely over what happened to your parents—the nightmares. I know it haunts you and makes you sensitive to...things. But I also know you, and I've seen you follow your gut before. I've never known it to lead you astray, never known you to go after something half-cocked."

"But..."

"Well, you know it's not much to go on right now; otherwise, you'd be telling the FBI about it instead of me. I think you need something more concrete."

"I know I do, but where am I going to get more evidence? Dr. Silverman is a foremost expert on WHISPs and he doesn't know jack about them. Besides, he certainly hasn't been doing his testing on serial killer WHISPs, more like people who are trying to cope with having them."

Finishing off her wine, Kristina clears her throat and draws back her shoulders. "I, um, might be able to help you with that."

"How?"

"There's a guy I used to date when I was still living in New Jersey. We broke up when I found out he was part of an underground anti-WHISP organization. He was only involved in recruiting, but he once mentioned his organization was 'digging into' WHISPs and what they really were, etcetera. Now, maybe he didn't know what the hell he was talking about, and it's not like we're talking about scientific research, but maybe they could help at least get you a solid lead on where to find more information."

"Why do you think they'd help me? If they're shady, they're not going to want to spill their guts to a cop."

"If they know you're the detective who put away Rachel Chester, they might talk to you. I mean, think about it, if you tell them you're investigating another case where the suspect has a WHISP, they might see this as an opportunity to show the world that WHISPs are evil. Now, it probably wouldn't be a great idea to tell them that you think a WHISP is killing people..." The edges of Kristina's lips curl in a small smile.

"Do you still have this guy's contact info?"

"Yeah, sadly I do. Very occasionally he sends me flyers for anti-WHISP rallies and stuff. I should've blocked his e-mails, but you know how lazy I am sometimes."

My echoing smile quickly fades.

"What?"

"I just had a thought. If the FBI finds out I'm contacting an anti-WHISP organization while working a high-profile case, I'm going to be in a shit-ton of trouble."

"What're they going to do? Fire you?"

CHAPTER 23

"After the third anti-WHISP bullying incident, we had to withdraw her from school, and after about three months she wouldn't leave the house anymore. The doctors were clueless, and we just didn't know where else to turn."

Excerpt: My Daughter is Not a Monster

It only takes a day for Kristina to set up the meet with her old beau's group. It's called CAW, Citizens Against WHISPs, and when I do a little digging into their reputation, shady doesn't quite cover it. The organization was international, if you counted branches in Canada, and was implicated in various crimes ranging from intimidation to kidnapping and murder. In no way was it a good idea for me to be going to talk to them alone and without backup, but I needed answers and didn't see any other options for getting them. I had two contingences in place: one, if I didn't call Kristina by an agreed time, she was to notify Crone of where I'd gone, and two, if anyone found out about the meeting, I'd say I'd gotten an anonymous tip they might be involved somehow, but given my history, I'd wanted to check them out on the down low first before more rumors got started. Both safety nets were admittedly flimsy, but every minute ticking by was a minute nearer to another murder and I didn't have time to set up better ones.

When I drive up, the meeting site, a non-descript warehouse in the Bronx, owned by a holding company, does not fill me with good vibes. I park on the street and apply the car's alarm, not because I think that anyone will care about a car alarm going off in this neighborhood, but because tripping it will disable the ignition. It's an older model Ford Focus, so it shouldn't be terribly appealing for car thieves for stripping, and there isn't anything to steal inside. Still, no sense in asking for trouble.

From the outside, the warehouse gives the impression of casual vacancy. Weeds erupt through cracks in the surrounding concrete, one of the ground floor windows is boarded up, and the mailbox post has an address spray-painted on it but lacks a mailbox. However, there are subtle signs of maintenance. While the chains on the several gates are old and rusty, each sports a shiny, new lock. Additionally, I spot a few repaired windows and a newer-looking security camera over the main door. Also raising my suspicions of occupancy, the windows have a reflective coating, making it impossible to see inside.

I've been instructed to use a side door and ring a buzzer. I comply and am rewarded with the answering buzz and click of the door unlocking. Having an itching desire to draw my gun, I turn the knob and push the door open. Inside is dark save the grey light from the grey day peeking in through the open door. I can't see much of the interior, and over thirty years of police training are screaming at me not to go inside. Ignoring training, I step up but keep a hand on the edge of the door, unwilling to let it fall shut.

"Hello?"

"Back here, Detective."

I'd expected such a shadowy organization to have a gravelly-voiced spokesperson, but the voice carrying down the hallway is a woman's, light and airy. Maybe I shouldn't, but I drop my guard and release the door. Once it shuts, a light comes on overhead. The hallway has a concrete floor and metal walls but is dust and cobweb free. I walk toward the source of the voice and find an office with a functional, though cleared, metal desk and a metal file cabinet. A strawberry blonde woman of average height in a grey skirt suit is in the process of locking the file cabinet when I arrive at the door. Gorgeous in a sharp, meticulous way, she's clearly used to making both men and women uncomfortable with her appearance, the blouse beneath her suit leaving little to the imagination by way of décolletage.

"Sorry, I had some paperwork to finish. Lila Grant."

"Detective Sylvia Harbinger."

We shake hands politely and I have to remind myself this woman is part of a group who probably murders people. I meet her grey eyes briefly then scan the room again. Seeing no chair other than the one behind the desk, I'm wondering how the interview is going to work when she waves a hand toward the door.

"Shall we?"

I follow her down the hallway and up a flight of spiral metal stairs to the second floor and another hallway. Roughly halfway down, there's an open door which she enters. This office is much cozier, with a large window, which, on any other day, would be basking sunlight onto a large wooden desk with a high-backed velvet desk chair. A typical black and red chevron-patterned rug and two black leather chairs complete the furnishings. Mentally, I note CAW's financials seem intact if not flush. Lila sits behind the desk and I take a chair in front.

"Now, I'm given to understand you have some questions about WHISPs."

"I do. I need to know more about how WHISPs interact

with their humans, how far away they can drift from them, how the particles are affected by human thought and other factors, that sort of thing."

"Mmmmm, and I have your word these questions are not officially part of any police investigation or action and you are asking them solely as a concerned citizen."

Must not roll eyes. "Right."

"Also, these personal questions are not in regard to any activities CAW may or may not engage in, and anything I say cannot be used against either myself or CAW."

"Ye—"

"Further, if I explain to you how any of the information I disclose was obtained, it will be assumed this 'how' was enacted by a separate entity."

My molars grind together. "Fine."

"I'll need your signature on this document." She slides a paper across her desk along with a pen.

I skim through it then sign it and slide it back to her. "Thorough."

Glancing at the signature, she then slips the document into a folder. "Should be. I'm a lawyer." She looks up at me. "Right, now that's taken care of, I believe your first question was asking about the length of the tether."

"Yes."

"You are assuming, of course, there is an actual physical tether between source human and WHISP. All of our...all evidence in this group's opinion points to the contrary. There have been recorded instances where a WHISP was able to be separated from its source human by hundreds of miles and still remain intact."

Shit. "But I thought the human's magnetic field was what kept the WHISP together."

Lila shakes her head. "A common misconception. Once

formed, the WHISP is nearly autonomous from the source human."

"So WHISPs can just wander around without their humans? Why don't people know that? Why have I never seen one do that? Why do the ones I've seen stay so close and only move when the human moves?"

"I've...the recorded instances I spoke of were under experimental conditions. Most WHISPs are caught up in the magnetic field of their host and forced to mimic their movements, but once separated by, oh say, six and a half feet, some then exhibit independent movement or movement directed by other outside influences."

I grip the arms of the chair to keep from shivering. "What outside influences and how did you experimentally separate a WHISP from its source human? I was told it couldn't be done."

"Nonsense. Separating WHISP from human is just a matter of introducing a very strong magnetic field to pull the WHISP particles away, or introducing a sufficient electromagnetic barrier between human and WHISP. And as for influences, we've se—heard of other humans weakly influencing separated WHISPs, high voltage power lines, electromagnets, large computers...well, I think you get the idea."

"Does it hurt?"

A tiny crease appears between her slim brows. "Does what hurt?"

"Ripping a WHISP away from a human by force. Does it hurt the person?"

"I already told you there isn't an actual physical tether."

"That's not an answer."

Her eyes narrow. "Yes. It hurts. Significantly."

CHAPTER 24

"The officer involved in the shooting of an unarmed man with a WHISP was acquitted of all charges today after the jury agreed with the defense's claims the man threatened the officer and tried to flee the scene. This is the fourth incidence of alleged anti-WHISP violence by Las Vegas police officers in the past six months."

Fox Local News at 7 Las Vegas

"BUT IF THERE'S NO PHYSICAL TETHER, THAN WHY would it hurt?"

Lila sighs. "Personally, I'd say it's psychosomatic, but it's theorized since some of the WHISP particles come from the source human, the loss of the electrical input from those particles triggers a pain response." Her eyes flicker away from mine and she licks her lips. "Also, there's other repercussions of the forced separation."

"What do you mean, repercussions?"

She folds her hands on top of her desk and her gaze returns to my face. "The separation may damage the source human."

A chasm opens up in my chest. "Damage? What kind of damage?"

"Psychological...perhaps neurological."

I open my mouth, but Lila sighs heavily and continues, "A source human which has been forcibly separated from its WHISP for extended periods of time may exhibit clinical signs of post-traumatic stress and certain, how shall I say, neurologic deficits."

"Brain damage?"

"Well, I wouldn't put it quite that dramatically, but I guess you could say that."

"You've done this to people? What the hell's wrong with you?"

Lila's mouth all but disappears in an angry, thin line.

"Now, now, Detective, you've already signed a document stating nothing I say here should or can be considered incriminating in any supposed criminal offense. I am merely answering your questions as a courtesy, one I can revoke at any time."

Wrathful blood rushes into my cheeks. I would love to slap handcuffs onto this smug woman's wrists right now, but I'm alone here, without backup, and legally, I'm on very thin ice. Also, I still need answers and I don't know anywhere else to get them. "Okay, so let me just do a little recap here. There is no physical tether connecting a WHISP to a human."

"Right."

"And WHISPs can therefore be separated from their humans and experimentally have been separated up to hundreds of miles without the WHISP dissipating, but it's painful and... damaging for the human."

"True."

My train of thought derails. *What if Chester was damaged by WHISP separation before she became a killer? She was found competent to stand trial. Still...* My stomach twists into a knot of uncertainty and I have to swallow back the lump of guilt in my throat. "How long before damage occurs? You said an extended period of time, what's extended?"

"It probably varies person to person, but we've seen significant damage begin within an hour."

"An hour, okay." Getting back on track. "And WHISPs separated more than six feet no longer move in response to their humans, but are influenced by other electromagnetic forces."

"Six and a half feet, but yes."

It's a lot of disturbing information to process, but it isn't answering my main questions. "And, have you ever seen a WHISP moving without a clear outside influence affecting it?"

"Yes."

"Why would it do that? Could it be moving because of residual, um, like thought energy from the human?"

"It seems plausible, but also WHISPs have been shown to shed particles in places they spend a lot of time, a person's residence for example, and they're sometimes drawn to these shed particles." Straightening a notepad on her desk, she clears her throat. "Of course, there are other interpretations."

I'm afraid to ask but I have to, "What other interpretations?"

"Oh, well, this is a less scientific area, with lots of semi-scientific overtones, but to simplify, some people feel WHISPs are sentient entities capable of moving and acting on their own volition without needing outside influences."

"That would be terrifying."

When Lila's mouth quirks up with approval at my remark, I regret saying it.

"Exactly. Hence the formation of CAW."

"But, it would only *really* be terrifying if the WHISPs were able to do anything. I mean, they're just clouds of particles, it's not like anything they do actually has an effect." But I already know this for the lie it is. I have the report on my desk from the phone company.

"Doesn't it?"

"What are you saying?"

"Are you aware there has been a ten-fold increase in poltergeist activity since the WHISP phenomenon started?"

"Well, I know at first the paranormal community thought they were ghosts and people tried exorcising them."

She rolls her eyes. "People still think that and there is a quite lucrative business in WHISP exorcisms, but what I'm talking about is the poltergeist activity associated with some ghosts. You know, like what was recorded in Amityville."

"And you think WHISPs are responsible for this increase in poltergeists?"

"I do. I've seen it."

"You've seen what?"

"I've seen a WHISP move things"—spine stiff, Lila closes her eyes and frowns—"known people who felt WHISPs touch them."

"People have felt a WHISP?"

Opening her eyes, Lila cocks her head. "Have you never noticed people who have WHISPs avoid contact with other WHISPs? They never walk through them as a normal human might do. Do you know why that is?"

I couldn't say I had ever really noticed it, but then I thought back to the WHISP clubs. Crone had stepped right through a few people's WHISPs, but the patrons had seemed very careful about touching others' WHISPs. "No, why?"

"Because they can feel the other person's WHISP, feel the particles acting on them. Normal people can't feel it."

"Why not?"

Folding her hands, she leans back in her chair. "Perhaps it's because having a WHISP makes you sensitive to other WHISPs, opens you up to the particles passing through you. Normal humans seem to have a natural barrier to WHISP particles. Maybe that's why they don't have WHISPs themselves already.

Now, of course, we don't know all people without WHISPs cannot feel them, because people can develop a WHISP at any age, but it stands to reason some people would have an innate immunity."

"What happens when WHISPs mix with other WHISPs?"

"They don't. What appears to happen when WHISPs overlap is the particle cloud's shape distorts to avoid the particles touching one another. They repel each other like magnets with the same polarity."

"You're telling me WHISPs can…touch objects and humans, but they can't touch other WHISPs?"

"Not in my experience."

Reeling, I'm struck dumb. I don't know what I wanted her to say. What she's saying is validating everything I've been thinking since I met with Dr. Silverman, yet also making me feel like I'm going insane. If she'd said WHISPs couldn't stray from their humans and they absolutely couldn't act on the physical world, then I wouldn't be feeling this empty, awful horror eating into my chest, but it would confirm I was losing sight of reality. Still, I have to remind myself where this information is coming from. Why should I trust CAW? It would be in their best interest to lie or, at least, stretch the truth about WHISPs to further their agenda of hatred and fear.

Lila is watching me closely. Almost as if she has read my mind, she presses her lips together. "You don't believe me."

"It's a lot to swallow, and it's not like CAW is a reputable scientific institution."

"You're not wrong. I have proof, but I don't think that CAW would be comfortable with me sharing it with an officer of the law, so I'm afraid you'll have to draw your own conclusions, Detective."

There is nothing about Lila Grant signaling her a liar, no tapping fingers, no straying of the eyes to the left-hand side, no hesitations or uneven speech, and no sheen of sweat or pulsing veins. But all this only means one of two things: one, she's a good poker player or two, she believes what she's saying. Being a detective, you get to understand the difference between someone telling the truth and someone thinking they're telling the truth. I needed a lot more, but I wasn't going to get it from CAW.

"Well, I guess that's it, then. Thank you for your time, Ms. Grant." I stand and offer a parting handshake.

Seeming a bit surprised, Lila also rises and sidles around to the front of the desk to shake my hand. "I hope you find what you're looking for, Detective."

And I almost hope I'm wrong about everything. "Thank you."

CHAPTER 25

"In an emergency meeting held yesterday at the UN headquarters in Manhattan, the Committee on WHISP Affairs condemned the slaying of hundreds of individuals with WHISPs in several countries, including Syria, Turkey, and Bangladesh. The committee is calling for leaders of those countries to work harder to put a stop to these anti-WHISP terrorist groups under threat of possible economic sanctions."

CNN

"WE GOT A BREAK!"

"Hmmm?" I'm comparing autopsy reports from the original victims to the copycat victims when Crone waddles up.

"Vice has an officer who's working on mob ties to one of our WHISP clubs. He's positive he's heard a group of regulars talking about the Chester case and we're in the process of tracking down names through credit card slips."

"Oh. Oh good. That's great."

Crone goes from elated to grumpy in two point three seconds. "Oh, well don't sound so freakin' excited about the first real break we've had in this case." Picking up a file off my desk he scans it. "You got somethin' from autopsy you're not telling me about?"

I snatch back the folder. "No, not really. I'm just double-checking the TODs and murder weapons."

"You mean the lack of murder weapons. I'm sure I don't have to tell *you* they never found one."

"Whaaaaaat?" I give him a seething look. "Of course, I know that. The forensic pathologist couldn't narrow it down except to say it was sharp and the killer was likely left-handed. I'm looking at the copycat murders. The wounds of Alice Petrie and William Rocks have subtle differences and his wounds suggest a right-handed assailant."

"Well, that makes complete sense. One of the copycats didn't get things exactly right."

"What about Pamela Cistern?"

"What about her?"

I lift up her file and point to several highlighted lines. "Her wounds are consistent with the original murders, not the copycat."

Wrinkles form along Crone's forehead, but then he shrugs. "So what? We know the same killer couldn't have killed them both."

"Okay, two copycats, a cult, whatever, fine. But then why would one mimic the crime so much closer than the other?"

"Maybe..."—the wrinkles reappear—"maybe there's only one weapon and they gave it to the only cult member who's left-handed?"

"If *we* don't know what the weapon is, how could the copycat know?"

"Easy, Chester told them what it was, or maybe gave it to them."

"When? While we had her under surveillance, before we

arrested her? When we were tracking every single one of her e-mails and phone calls?"

Face red, Crone flings Cistern's folder down on my desk. "Before that."

"And she just happened to have the foresight to do it before we were onto her."

"I don't know, Harbinger. What do you want? How about we ask them when vice is done rounding them up for us?"

"You think it'll be that easy?"

"I don't think anything, as long as the killings stop." He turns away. "I'll let you know when we're ready to start interviews."

Watching Crone stalk off, I'm wondering if I should have tried acting more excited, but I don't have a whole lot of time to worry about Crone's delicate feelings. Right now, I'm struggling with my own. All of the victims had a WHISP, so if what I learned from CAW is true, they could've been killed by a WHISP. If even some of the original victims were killed by a WHISP, it means they weren't killed by Rachel Chester, and if they weren't killed by Rachel Chester, I may have put an innocent woman in jail. It's something I'm not willing to cope with right now. Chester is a high functioning, paranoid schizophrenic who was found mentally capable of standing trial, blood from two of the victims was found in her apartment, on her shoes and on her clothes, and she had no solid alibi for any of the murders. The defense's only explanation for the presence of the blood, was Chester had assaulted both of the victims before their murders. It was a flimsy argument and it didn't hold.

Chester was convicted, but I'd always wondered about the murder weapon. Sure, there had been other cases where we never found the weapon, but there had always been a clear indication of what the murder weapon had been: three-inch serrated knife, tire iron, twenty-two hunting rifle. In the

Chester case, cause of death was always exsanguination due to sharp force trauma inflicted by an unknown object. What if the "unknown object" was Ray? Then Chester was guilty, right? Only she'd used her WHISP as a weapon. If she was able to control the particles somehow, or get Ray close enough to the victim and then mime the attack? Right now, the evidence only proved she was present when the victims were killed, it was a long way from proving Chester killed them with her WHISP. In fact, I'm certain it isn't possible to prove it.

My temples are pounding and I down two Excedrin. *Fuck.* If I really think it's Chester killing people through Ray, then I have to get twenty-four seven eyes on Chester. Right now, she's monitored outside of her cell, and there's a camera inside her cell, but there isn't someone watching just her feed all the time. Also, since she doesn't receive any unmonitored communications and doesn't interact with the general prison community, I don't have any basis to ask for constant monitoring or to subpoena the footage. My frustration bubbles over, then doubt floods in again and my brain roils. Chester's original victims, as far as I could get from her, were men with WHISPs she saw on the street and thought were out to get her.

Originally, I'd sympathized with her for being afraid of other people's WHISPs even though she seemed comfortable with Ray, but now I wonder if it was actually that she somehow knew WHISPs could hurt her. Regardless, she had seen the men on the street. If she and Ray are still killing now, how are they finding victims? Rachel Chester's in solitary confinement. She doesn't have a television in her cell and her time on the prison computers is short and strictly monitored. The new victims aren't celebrities and she only knew Pamela Cistern. I can buy Chester using Ray as a weapon when she's standing right there, but could she send her out to kill a random person? And if so, why wouldn't Ray kill the first person she...*it* came upon? It's a possibility. Still, it's unlikely Ray wandered so far from Rikers without crossing paths with someone who had a WHISP. There had to be something more to it.

I decide to start at the beginning of the new cases, Alice Petrie. If Chester met her in some random encounter on the street, there was nothing I could do to make the connection, but I'm going to dig as deep as I can to make sure there is no other connection from Chester to Petrie. When Alice Petrie was killed, we'd kept the connection between her death and Chester's MO on the down low because we were afraid of copycat panic, and also to deny the copycat the publicity. Keeping that in mind, interviews with neighbors had specifically not mentioned Chester. Well, the copycat was out of the bag now, so I'm going to interview all her relatives, friends, and neighbors again.

Halfway to the elevator, I turn around and head past my desk to Crone's. He doesn't look up when I approach.

"Hey, listen, I want to go back and interview Alice Petrie's family and friends. Neighbors, too."

Crone grunts. "Why?"

"When we interviewed them the first time, we were careful not to mention Chester. Now that we're not suppressing the copycat from the press, I want to interview them again and double check any connections Petrie might have had to Chester."

Finally looking up, he clicks his tongue. "And now we're partners again?"

"What do you mean?"

"Gimme a little credit, Harbinger, I'm a detective, too. You've been off on your own crusade for a few days now. You gonna let me in on it?"

I chew my lower lip. "Maybe, but are you in for this?"

Closing a folder, he sighs. "Yeah sure, all right."

CHAPTER 26

"Thousands of WHISPers supported by family and friends gathered for a WHISP-Pride rally in the Castro District of San Francisco earlier today. The message: WHISPs are not a Choice."

San Francisco Tribune

WE HIT THE PHONES, SET UP INTERVIEWS WITH ALICE Petrie's friends and family, and then get in the car. I'm wondering if we'll run into Mike and if I'll be able to recognize his voice. Alice lived in a smaller apartment building squeezed between four taller ones, and I'm looking up trying to figure out which of the adjacent ones has the best view of Petrie's window. There are too many that could be home to the anonymous caller. *Damn.* We're starting in Petrie's building, anyway. Crone leads the way but holds the door open for me after we get buzzed in by her next-door neighbor, one of only three neighbors on Petrie's floor.

Bypassing the broken elevator, we take the stairs up to the third floor and I wait for Crone at the landing to hold the door for him. When he catches up, I bite back a comment on his fitness level, and walk next to him down past the crime scene, unlucky 313, to the door just beyond, apartment 315. I knock. Mrs. Gladys Long, a seventy-seven-year-old widow with a walker and long grey hair answers promptly.

"Hello Mrs. Long, thank you so much for agreeing to speak with us again."

"Well, I don't know what else I can tell you detectives. I was soundly asleep and I didn't hear anything until the woman who car pools with her started screaming, but come in. Can I get you some tea?"

"No, thank you."

"I'm fine."

We follow her into a tiny living room and are swallowed up once more by her ancient green velvet sofa. Gladys herself eases down into the matching club chair.

"Well, what did you want to ask me?"

Crone scoots forward to answer. "We're still investigating Ms. Petrie's murder, and we've linked it to another series of murders. Do you recognize this woman?" He produces Chester's photo from a folder and holds it up for Mrs. Long to examine.

"Let me get my glasses on here." She snags a pair of eyeglasses on a beaded chain around her neck and puts them on. "Hmmmm. Can I see it closer?"

He relinquishes the photo, and she holds it up inches from her face.

"She does look familiar."

He sighs. "From the television?"

"No. I think she might have lived here in this building, maybe even in Alice's apartment. Now this would've been a few years ago, and she didn't live here very long, wasn't very social."

My heart's beating so fast it hurts. "Are you sure?"

Handing back the photo, Gladys eyes me over her glasses.

"Well, as sure as I can be at my age. Can't you find out for sure yourselves?"

Crone smirks. "Yes, yes we can."

"Thank you again for you time, Mrs. Long."

"Is that all you needed?" She's frowning me down.

"Have you seen the woman recently? Was she friends with Alice?"

"No, I don't think so. I haven't seen her in a long time here and I don't think she and Alice were friends."

Crone takes over. "Have you seen any of the woman's old friends hanging around or talking with Alice?"

"No. That lady didn't have many friends."

I think of something else. "Have you noticed any strange people hanging around, specifically people with WHISPs?"

Gladys scratches her head. "Well, lots of people around here have WHISPs. Alice had one herself, but she was still very friendly. Not at all like that other girl."

"I'm sorry, but I have to ask, are you familiar at all with the Rachel Chester case?"

Wincing at my question, Crone glances at me sidelong but doesn't say anything.

"Oh, yeah, the whole serial killer thing. You know, come to think of it, that killer lady looks an awful lot like the woman who used to live in Alice's apartment…" Her eyes widen. "Oh, my goodness! That's the same woman, isn't it?"

I have to come clean with Mrs. Long now. "I'm sorry, we'll have to do some checking, but we think so."

"Poor Alice's death is part of the copy killer thing then? Oh, that's just dreadful. I don't understand how people can be so awful." Gladys rubs her wrinkled hands together.

Crone tries to squeeze for just a little more. "Is there anything else you can remember about Rachel Chester when she was living here? Do you remember any of her friends or relatives? Anything you can remember would be very helpful."

"Um...no, I'm sorry."

Producing a card, Crone manages to escape the couch and rise. "If you think of anything, here's my card."

With difficulty, I also stand. "Call any time."

Gladys shows us to the door and the deadbolt snaps into place as soon as she closes it. We have two other neighbors left to interview on this floor alone, but this is huge, so I yank out my cell and call Hines, one of the junior detectives working the case.

"Hines here."

"Harbinger. Listen, I need you to track down previous leases for Alice Petrie's apartment."

"How far back?"

"Go five years if you have to."

"Am I looking for something in particular?"

"Yeah, Rachel Chester."

———

MOST OF THE OTHER TENANTS HAVEN'T LIVED THERE as long as Mrs. Long and don't remember Chester ever living there. It's closing in on six when we finish up and Crone waits until we're back in the car to grill me.

"How'd you know we'd find a connection to Chester?"

"I didn't really, but I had a hunch there could be one."

"Is it because of Pamela Cistern?"

I'm trying to rub the weariness out of my eyes. "Huh?"

"Chester's original victims were random, but the copycat is killing people with connections to her."

"Maybe. Kinda looks that way."

Scratching his stubble, Crone's face scrunches up. "Seems odd though. How would the copycat know about places where Chester used to live? Seems like a weird thing to mention to someone. I mean, you might tell someone you once lived in Soho, but you wouldn't give them the exact address."

"Could just be someone who knew Chester a few years ago and went to her house. She could have, or, at least, *had* friends we don't know about."

"Yeah, I guess." By the way Crone says it, he knows I'm still not telling him everything.

CHAPTER 27

"The suit against the town of Blevins, Arkansas, is now
headed to the supreme court. Several WHISPers are
suing the town which is a self-proclaimed WHISP-free
zone."

Arkansas Daily Online

WHAT IS OBVIOUS TO ME NOW IS THE VICTIMS AREN'T
the connection, the places are. It makes sense Chester's WHISP
couldn't randomly wander around without the particles just
dispersing. Ray would have to be drawn to something and
being drawn to a location which had some of Chester's residual
energy or something seemed likely. We hadn't bothered to look
into other places Chester had lived before since her DNA didn't
match any unsolved crimes and no unsolved crimes outside of
New York had her MO. It didn't seem relevant to the case, but
now it is.

Crone and I are both digging into all of her residences when
I'm once again summoned by Agent Coppola. This time as I
stroll over to his office in records, I'm much calmer, but when I
reach the door and raise my fist to knock, the door swings open

before I can. The chief is leaving Coppola's office and when his gaze meets mine, I know I'm in deep shit. Without a word, the chief ushers me into the office and shuts the door behind me. Swallowing hard, I sit and prepare for what I thought was coming last time I was in the office, because this time Coppola's cheeks are flushed and his jaw is set. I search my brain for answers to how I screwed the pooch and how I can justify it.

"Detective Harbinger, I've heard you've been doing a little research project."

"Well, yeah, Crone and I just got back from interviewing Alice Petrie's neighbors again. I felt we needed to—"

"That's not what I'm talking about."

"Oh?" *Oh shit.*

"I'm talking about a solo side project you've been undertaking. Does the acronym C-A-W mean anything to you?"

A part of me wants to lie very badly because not only should I have not, under any circumstances, gone to speak to anyone at CAW without authorization, I certainly shouldn't have done it without any backup. Also, there is a strong probability Coppola will think I'm nuts when I tell him I think a WHISP is murdering people. Unfortunately, it's one thing to hold back the whole truth from Crone but another thing entirely to lie to the face of the FBI agent in charge of your case. I'm stuck between a rock and an avalanche of rocks. *Fuck.*

"Sir, I can explain."

"That's nice. I don't want to hear it. Clearly, you have WHISP issues and have chosen the middle of a very sensitive and highly public case to explore them. So, I'm sorry, Detective Harbinger, but the FBI and the NYPD thank you for your assistance on this case, but your consulting services are no longer needed—"

"But I—"

"Do you really want me to have you escorted from the building?"

I open my mouth again, then close it. Screaming at an FBI agent is an even worse plan then lying to one. I stand, then turn and leave the office with as much dignity as being subtly called a lunatic and tossed off a case can afford. When I've collected my briefcase and cleared the borrowed desk of my belongings, I pay Crone a visit. He doesn't seem to notice anything amiss although I hold my coat and briefcase.

"So, I think I tracked down another room Chester rented, but there's a gap where she listed her address as a P.O. Box, and it's no longer registered to her."

"That's great, Crone, I'll e-mail you what I have so far."

Finally, he takes a good look at me. "What's going on?"

"Coppola kicked me off the case. Call me when you finish up tonight and we'll have a beer." I turn to head to the elevator, but Crone jumps up and grabs my shoulder.

"What the hell? We just had two huge breaks in the case. Is this some kind of sick joke?"

"Do I look like I'm laughing?"

"Screw this, I'm gonna go tell Agent Coppola to go fuck himself."

I'm touched by his anger, but I can't let Crone blindly defend me to Coppola. "Hey, I appreciate it, really I do, but just don't, at least not until we have that beer. You, ah, you might think differently afterwards."

He sets his jaw. "I've never seen you do anything but work your ass off to solve this case, and after Chester, I wouldn't have blamed you if you'd've told NYPD to go fuck themselves. What the fuck could you have possibly done?"

Crone isn't whispering, so roughly half the department is now watching us. "Not here. Meet me at Dead Rabbit Lucky's, ten o' clock. I'll...I'll tell you everything."

Looking like someone kicked his puppy, he relents. "Fine. You better."

I nod and head toward the elevator, deliberately avoiding

eye contact with anyone else and wondering if this is the last time I'll be walking out of the precinct.

————

WHEN I GET HOME, BEN'S ON THE COUCH WATCHING television, but turns it off and bolts to the door. "What happened?"

At first, I think he's already heard something about my getting kicked off the case, but then I realize I'm home a lot earlier than usual. I open my mouth to speak, but my eyes prickle and my voice gets snagged in my throat. Ben throws his arms around me.

"They didn't make you go interview Chester again after what happened, did they?"

"No. Actually, they threw me off the case."

Ben lets me go. "What?"

"Can we sit down?"

"'Course."

Ben pours me a glass of water and waits on the couch while I get out of my coat and shoes. When I eventually sit beside him, his face is carefully neutral, but his eyes give away his relief. I take a sip of water. This man is my husband, my soul-mate, if I believed in that stuff, and he's been through a lot of shit husbands not married to cops don't have to go through. I love him like mad, yet I don't know if I can tell him about this, about the real reason I've been kicked off the case.

Ben's a physicist, everything in his world is neat and explainable with math. He took the WHISP phenomenon almost without blinking once he thought he understood the physics of it all. I've told him about what happened the night my parents were murdered and how WHISPs remind me of that night. He knows the stuff of my nightmares, and he's willing to move away from this city with me even if it means leaving

Lincoln to finish his last two years of school alone. Still, I'm afraid. I'm afraid he's tired of walking on eggshells for me and that he's disappointed, even with therapy, I can't be rational about WHISPs.

What if I'm wrong about what's going on? Kristina didn't think I was crazy to think a WHISP could kill someone, but not thinking I was insane and thinking I was right are two different things. Also, she's not a scientist like Ben, with a rigid mind ruled by logic. He'll want proof I don't have and don't know how to get. And if he doesn't believe me and thinks I'm falling deeper into my neurosis, if he thinks I'm starting to convince myself all people with WHISPs must be evil, then what will he think I believe about our own son when he already imagines I'm running away from Lincoln and his WHISP? But I can't lie to Ben, either. He'd know, and he'd resent it even if I was lying to not push him and Lincoln further away. *But how to begin?*

"I've been doing some investigation on the case on my own without authorization or back-up."

He frowns, not because he thinks I should've been following procedure, but probably because he's pissed I didn't tell him what I was doing. "What kind of investigation?"

"A WHISP investigation."

CHAPTER 28

"The appearance of a WHISP does not indicate and should not be construed as a sign of an underlying medical condition."

The Implications of Disease in Patients with a WHISP by Dr. Naomi Glaskov

BY HIS EXPRESSION, BEN'S TRYING TO UNDERSTAND, but I see exasperation there. "Why would you be doing that now?"

"I was following a lead."

"What lead?"

Unable to hold his gaze, I look past him to the window. "We got a call from an anonymous eyewitness who said he'd seen a WHISP in the victim's apartment the night she died."

"So what? All the victims had WHISPs right?"

"It wasn't her WHISP."

Ben opens his mouth, then closes it again, swallowing down a look of frustration. "Okay."

"It got me thinking the killer could also have a WHISP, so I did some research."

"That was just following the evidence of the case, I don't see why you wouldn't be authorized to do it."

"Well"—I clear a hitch in my throat—"it wasn't just that."

"All right, what was it then?"

"I spoke to this WHISP researcher, Dr. Silverman, and there were things he said that got me to thinking...about other things, about how much we don't know about WHISPs. I needed more information, so I...went to talk to someone less reputable about WHISPs."

Ben's fist clenches. "Who?"

"CAW."

"Jesus, Sylvy. Why would you talk to people like that? Especially without backup? Those people are zealots, not to mention kidnappers and murderers."

"I told you, I needed more information."

"What kind of information?"

This is it, and I can't sit still. I stand and walk to the window. Outside, the city is going on as if the world isn't a new and terrifying place, as if everything is normal. Down on the street, none of the passersby have WHISPs, and I can almost convince myself the past few years haven't happened. "I needed to know what WHISPs are really capable of."

Ben is silent for several beats. "What do you mean by that? WHISPs aren't capable of anything, Sylvy, they're just some electromagnetic waves which got caught up around a person. You know that."

"What I know, is they're made of particles, and those particles respond to electromagnetic impulses. People already know they mess with cell phones sometimes, that's being capable of something. Why couldn't they be capable of more?"

"What are you saying?"

Steeling myself, I turn to face him. "I'm not saying WHISPs are alive with their own thoughts and feelings, but I am saying they interact with the world, more than we think they do, or maybe it's a matter of them strengthening over time and being able to do more. It usually only takes them a few weeks or months to develop, so it makes sense they wouldn't stay the same over time. The point is, I think Chester is using hers as a weapon."

Shaking his head, Ben is up and in front of me in seconds. I despise the pitying twist of his mouth, the fear in his eyes. He brushes a hair from my forehead and then cradles my cheek in his hand.

"Babe, that's not possible. Chester's in prison. She can't hurt anyone anymore. How could she?"

"WHISPs can separate from their source humans." Or rather, what I'd been told is they could *be* separated from a human, but I want what I'm saying to sound as plausible as possible to Ben.

"Who told you that? CAW? They'd say anything to make people afraid of WHISPs. The fact is, if a WHISP could separate from a person it would just dissipate. It's a human's...well, kind-of like a human's gravity which keeps all those wave-particles together."

It's clear nothing I say will make him believe me, he has science and my phobia on his side. His words are my fears manifested, and I'm struck speechless. After a few moments, Ben must at least sense he's playing with fire because he tries to steer away from directly opposing me.

"Well, maybe this is for the best. We agreed taking on the case was a bad idea and now maybe you don't have to feel guilty. You gave them everything you could to help with this case and if they won't let you help anymore, then what can you do?"

Now I'm mad. I'm mad at Ben for thinking this is a good thing, I'm mad at Coppola for not even giving me a chance to explain myself, but most of all, I'm mad at myself for being too afraid to commit to what I believe and bring forward my thoughts to Crone or Coppola before. Now I'm stuck on the outside looking in, knowing in my gut I'm right, but hoping I'm wrong and waiting for more people to die, and Ben not believing me is something I can't deal with right now. I push past him and head into the bedroom to change. "I'm going out."

"Sylvia, come on, don't leave. We don't have to talk about it anymore tonight, just don't go." He follows me into the bedroom. "Listen, I should've said this before. I'm sorry they kicked you off the case because I know how much it meant to you."

Ignoring him, I change into jeans and a sweatshirt.

"Will you at least let me apologize? You threw a lot at me. I'm sorry I'm not handling it well, but this is…a lot, and we're both very emotional right now."

I run a brush through my hair and check my appearance in the mirror.

"I'm sorry I'm happy I get my wife back, and we get to continue on with our life together. What do you want from me?"

"Right now, I just want some space."

I don't mean to sound so hard. Even though his not trusting me cuts into my heart, deep down I know he thinks he's doing the right thing. I love him and I don't want to throw away our marriage, which is why I need to cool off and think before we talk about it more. A drink won't hurt either. After putting on my shoes, I step out into the hallway.

"I'll be at Dead Rabbit Lucky's and I'll leave my cell on for emergencies, but please don't call or text unless you have to."

Right before the door shuts behind me, Ben stops it from closing. "I love you."

I want to say the words, really I do. It isn't fair to blame Ben for reacting exactly the way I thought he would, but still, I'm not ready to forgive him. "I know."

CHAPTER 29

"A new trend has surfaced on Facebook: the WHISP profile. The social media giant now allows WHISPers to set up a profile specifically for their WHISP, and thousands have taken advantage of the new feature."

"Latest from Facebook," Mashable.com

I HAIL A CAB, UNSURE WHETHER I'LL BE SOBER enough on the back end to drive myself home. Fortunately, the cabbie is too busy rocking out to some early 90s punk to engage in conversation. Staring out the window, rain begins to blur the passing city. Not for the first time, I think about how much I'm going to miss it, how lonely it'll be at the cabin. I'm hoping I will grow to love the solitude, but who am I kidding? *I'll fucking hate it.*

Dead Rabbit Lucky's is a decent bar in a seedy part of Hell's Kitchen. Ben and I used to frequent it after I'd solved a frustrating or upsetting case, back when a typical case could bother me. After around year ten as a detective, I'd thickened my skin and we'd stopped going, but I knew it was still there. As we pull up, I can make out the darkly humorous neon sign of a magician pulling a dead white rabbit, complete with x's for eyes, out of a black top hat, his expression transforming from smarmy confidence to horror.

After paying the driver, I hoof it to the door and only receive a mild soaking for my trouble. It's about an hour and a half shy of when I'm supposed to meet Crone, but the bar has free pretzels and popcorn, and I'm in the mood to drink alone for a while. Taking an empty seat at the almost filled bar, I make eye contact with the young, black, nose-ringed, spiky-haired bartender who gives me a nod and finishes up with a couple before heading over to me.

"What can I getcha?"

"A shot of tequila and a Fat Tire."

She nods. "That bad of a day, huh?"

"You could say that."

"Do you want to start a tab?"

"Yep."

I hand her my credit card and she takes it with a sympathetic smile.

"I'll grab you more pretzels too."

"That'd be great."

She returns shortly with the pretzels and beer, and then pours the tequila. I don't let the shot glass touch the bar.

"Salud."

I down the shot and hand her back the glass. Her lips part, but then a man a few patrons down waves at her enthusiastically and points to his empty glass in what I'm sure he thinks is a charming way. The bartender rolls her eyes at me and then floats over to him. It's for the best. I couldn't pour out my heart to her like in some feel-good movie of the week. I have to work out my own shit right now.

Sipping at the beer, I shove a couple of pretzels into my mouth and think while I chew. What I need is to figure out Chester's next victim before she gets out of the infirmary and isn't monitored twenty-four seven. The trouble is, even tracking down all of the places Chester ever lived, and possibly staking them out, doesn't guarantee anything. We might not be able to see Ray going in and, if we did, I have no idea how we'd stop her from killing. Well, that's not exactly true, something like an EMP or powerful electromagnet might do the trick, but they aren't things I have access to right now.

Okay, stopping Ray once she's at a location won't help, but maybe if we got the person away from the location? Right, so then we'd just have to ask a bunch of people to stay at a hotel indefinitely or, better yet, have them move out and not allow anyone to move back in. I take a long draw of beer then grab another handful of pretzels. I feel the warm ooze as the tequila hits my bloodstream via my empty stomach, and decide I'll just confuse myself and get frustrated trying to suss out a plan tonight. But it doesn't mean I'm stopping. Being kicked off the case and having no support from Ben is going to make things a whole hell of a lot harder, but screw it. Giving up isn't an option and never has been, and I've still got about two weeks on Ben and my original deal. I'll have to figure out other ways, that's all. And lie to Ben. *Shit.*

————

I'M TWO BASKETS OF PRETZELS AND THREE BEERS IN when Crone shows up. Unlike me, he hasn't been home to clean up and change and looks a lot like he slept in his clothes instead of spent the day in them. Spotting me, he frowns and marches up. "Couldn't have picked a nicer place, huh?"

"We have a history, Lucky's and I." I shift off the bar stool, only wobble slightly, and appropriate my beer and third pretzel basket from the bar. "Order a drink and meet me at the table in the corner."

Having learned to take Crone's grunt as assent, I leave him

and wend my way to the shadowy corner table in the back of the bar. I'm grateful but not surprised it's empty since most of tonight's action is up at the bar and there isn't any wait staff. I slide into the booth, pushing away memories of Ben and me at this table. Crone isn't far behind. As he sits, I point to the drink in his hand.

"I asked you to join me for a beer. That's not a beer."

"My favorite beer is Scotch."

"Fair enough." I sip at my fourth beer, but I'm full and on the edge of tipping over the fine line between drunkenness and puking.

Crone, on the other hand, takes a healthy gulp of his scotch. "Now talk."

"I fucked up."

"Thank you, Lieutenant Obvious. I'd already figured that one out, being a detective and all."

I dip a finger in my beer and swirl it around the rim of my glass. "I had a hunch and I was too much of a fucking coward to come out with it, so I skulked around on my own and I got caught."

"Got caught doing what exactly?"

I look him in the eye. "Researching WHISPs."

"Hmm." More of Crone's scotch finds its way into his stomach. "That makes sense."

"It does?"

"I couldn't think of anything which would piss the chief off so much he'd let Coppola kick you out, but anything that might drag the NYPD, and the FBI, for that matter, into another volley of ugly anti-WHISP publicity would do it."

Crone continues to surprise me with his insight. "Guess so."

"So, who'd you talk to that got everyone's panties in a bunch?"

"CAW."

Nearly spitting out a mouthful of scotch, Crone sputters, "Holy shit, Harbinger. That was ballsy."

"It was stupid."

"Then why do it?"

I'm feeling saucy, so I push the pretzel basket toward him. "You're a detective, why do you think I did it?"

Scrutinizing me, he chooses a pretzel and pops it into his mouth. "Well, you're a driven woman who can't let go, and a detective bent on justice. You wouldn't risk getting thrown off the case unless you had a damn good reason, and since we were already onto the theory the killer had a WHISP, it's something else."

I flick the side of my glass. "Bring it on home."

"You think the WHISP did it."

CHAPTER 30

Kitti60: "Jordan totally deserved that rose!!!!"

Luvly1: "I knw, right?"

HeyYou88: "The only rsn Katia didn't chse him was becse he had a WHISP."

The Bachelorette Forum, Thread: I "heart" Jordan

"Bingo."

Crone raises a single eyebrow in response.

"I'm not delusional. I don't think WHISPs fly around and murder people of their own volition. I think Chester is somehow using Ray to kill people."

He lets out a deep, wheezy breath and finishes off his scotch. "Well, I can see why you didn't want to bring this up to me and Coppola."

"Do you believe it's possible for a WHISP to kill someone?"

"You got some proof you're not telling me about?"

I swallow a mouthful of beer turned warm and bitter. "Nope."

"You got some way of getting proof?"

"Not really. Not yet."

"Fuck, Harbinger, you're not giving me a choice here. I can't believe it."

"You mean, you can't believe *me*."

"Listen, I know you're a good cop, and I know you've been turning yourself inside out trying to figure this case out, but maybe you need this step back to get some perspective."

"Think about it, Crone, why would we just assume all WHISPs are identical, that they would all act exactly the same? It doesn't make any sense the things wouldn't grow and change over time, become more attuned to their human's thoughts. I'm not even talking about telekinesis or anything, I'm talking about electrical impulses having an effect on a mass of particles. That's at least a little fucking scientific, isn't it?"

He outlines his mouth with his thumb and forefinger. "A little. But if Chester could kill people with her WHISP, then why hasn't she murdered the guards over at Rikers and made a break for it?"

"The woman at CAW said something about the particles only being able to affect people who also have WHISPs."

"And there's some kind of scientific explanation for that?"

"I'm sure there is, but I'm not a fucking particle physicist."

"Right, okay, point taken. But...aw crap, this is just too fucking weird. Just...let's just wait until we get this round of interviews with the suspects that vice rounded up for us done, okay? If those are a dead end then, fuck, I don't know, we'll figure something out."

I want to tell him not to do me any favors, but without Crone's help, I'll be completely out of the loop. "Fine. When are you starting those interviews?"

"Tomorrow."

"Keep me in the loop."

"Yeah, okay."

———

A GLARE IS CUTTING INTO MY RETINAS THROUGH MY closed eyelids as the world slowly comes back and my gut clenches and heaves, nausea spreading down from the back of my skull into my throat and stomach. Swallowing down bile with a dry and sour tongue, I roll onto my back and raise an arm to protect my eyes from the light. As far as I remember, I finished off the fourth beer and maybe two others before taking a cab home, and the current state of my head and stomach certainly seem to confirm it. I'm contemplating sitting up when I hear the bedroom door open and Ben's furtive movements. I could feign sleep, but thirst combined with a strong desire not to move triumphs over residual petty anger.

"I'm awake."

"Oh, okay, how are you feeling?"

"Abysmal. What time is it?"

"Almost one."

Slowly I tilt my arm so I can peer at him under it. "Crap."

He comes over and sits on the edge of the bed. "Don't worry about it, it's not like you have any place to be."

"No, I guess I don't."

"Do you wanna talk about it?"

I'm not sure if he means my drunken outing, our fight, my removal from the case, or my WHISP neurosis, so I shake my head. The world wubba-wubba's and I wince. "But I could use a nice big glass of water."

"I'll do you one better. I went out this morning and got some Gatorade."

"Perfect."

Ben exits and I slowly and painfully prop myself up into a non-choking position before he returns with a yellow Gatorade with a bendy straw sticking out of it. Despite my hangover and everything happening, I can't suppress a smile. Remembering a bendy straw is true love. He hands me the bottle and returns to sitting on the edge of the bed. I take a tentative sip and let the liquid spread out across my tongue before swallowing. It's sweet and salty and good, and I think I may avoid vomiting after all.

"What are you thinking in the food department?"

"Negatory."

"Do you want me to leave you alone for a bit?"

Despite still being mad at him, I can't shun him when he's taking such good care of me and my hangover. Also, he might need to hold my hair back. "No."

Ben's eyes roam around the bedroom as if he's searching for something to say. "I, ah, talked to Lincoln earlier today."

"What did you tell him?"

"I didn't tell him anything," his voice is tight. "I thought you'd want to talk to him yourself about…things. Maybe now… maybe you can have lunch with him this week."

"Maybe…" I haven't let myself really think about Lincoln lately, and the guilt is now leaching into me.

"He said things are going really well in the lab right now. He's excited about a project he'll be starting with the particle accelerator."

"That's great."

The elephant in the room seems to be crushing both of us, but I don't know what to say to Ben right now, and I can't think of anything but lies. "Did anyone call for me?"

His expression darkens. "No. Are you expecting a call?"

I shrug. "Crone promised to keep me in the loop."

"He did?"

"Call it a professional courtesy."

"Ah."

I'm nearly finished with the Gatorade and feeling decidedly more human. "Maybe I could go for brunch."

Watching as relief washes over him, for a moment the

horrible awkwardness between us is lifted. Ben leans forward and kisses me on the nose.

"You got it."

I let a smile spread across my lips, but as soon as he leaves, the smile fades. The degree to which my life is currently screwed up is astonishing.

CHAPTER 31

WHISPLite is a small, lightweight device that allows you to choose from seven different colors and eight different light pattern settings to make your WHISP stand out in the crowd.

WHISPLite Kickstarter campaign

BEN'S OUT GETTING GROCERIES, AND I'M IN THE office with ginger tea to calm my still delicate stomach, sorting out my facts. I'm doing it for Ben and Crone, but more for myself. I need to find a real way to move forward without waiting for another body to drop, but sometimes to move forward, we need to go back. I pull out my personal files on Rachel Chester's first victim, Michael Rose. Technically, we never found trace evidence to directly link her to his death, but the MO was so exact I never had a doubt he was her first.

As I'm flipping through the pages, reliving the crime scene in my mind, I feel like I'm caught in a spider web of Chester's creation. Over a year has passed and I am right back at the beginning, staring down at Michael Rose's remains and wishing I'd retired a year sooner. The first thing I'd taken note of then was the brutality of the murder. According to friends, family, and coworkers, Michael was an amiable divorcee who'd only recently developed a WHISP. No one could think of any enemies and the ex-wife, living in California with her new husband, had seemed shocked and upset when interviewed.

Yet the dismemberment of the body spoke to a degree of hate I'd rarely, if ever, witnessed as a homicide detective. I remember hoping we'd find shady dealings somewhere in his financials, or a drug problem—anything—to explain his death as something other than a random killing, because a random killing hinted of a serial killer. Then one lead after another withered and died until the only possibility was a random killing. Less than a month later, Chester struck again.

Her next victim was a married law clerk, Jeffrey Wales, but at the time of his murder, his wife was out of town visiting relatives. Even though it takes three victims to consider a murderer a serial killer, I already knew it was what we had. It didn't even phase me when we turned up evidence Jeffrey had a serious gambling problem, because I knew the lead would amount to nothing, and it did. The same MO to the letter, but this time we got lucky and found an out-of-place hair at the crime scene. Sadly, with no suspect yet, there was nothing to compare the hair to. It was only much later that we scored with a statistically significant correspondence of Chester's DNA to DNA recovered from the hair, but still, that evidence had ultimately amounted to squat due to a rooky technician mislabeling the chain of evidence sheet.

But really, according to my fucked up theory, there shouldn't be any evidence of Chester at the crime scenes. If she could just send out Ray to kill people and leave no evidence behind, why wouldn't she do that? The answer wasn't too hard to fathom: she wanted to be there. She wanted to see Ray murder those people. Or maybe her tether was shorter a year ago and she had to be there. In any case, I didn't think for one minute she was innocent in all this. She must have been controlling Ray, using her as a weapon. But was she controlling her now? *Oh, come on Sylvia, let's not even go there. Crone already thinks you're a loony bird.*

Oh God, Crone. Why the fuck did I go blabbing my theory to him last night? Was I really that desperate after getting thrown off the case? He's probably sitting his big blubbery ass on his desk right now with a bear claw in one hand, holding court and confirming everyone's suspicions I'm off my rocker when it comes to WHISPs. I can almost hear him laughing at me despite his trappings of humanity last night. Or maybe I'd just been too drunk to notice he was only pretending to give a shit, nodding with insincerity when I told him I'd wanted to be a cop years before my parents were murdered.

My stomach roils at the memory and I take another sip of tea. Nothing I can do about it now. The WHISP's out of the bag. I set aside the Wales file and move on to Jacob Beene's. I try to picture Chester frequenting the coffee shop, taking note of the only employee there with a WHISP. I wonder what he said to her to set her off. Did he try to befriend her? Maybe make some joke about getting Ray a chai latte? Or maybe he'd never even spoken to her. Chester never once mentioned a motive. It's possible the whole thing didn't have anything to do with Beene or Infante or Wilcox or any of them specifically. They might have just looked like men who'd once wronged her.

My head is aching in spite of the Tylenol I popped earlier. I'm not even sure what I'm doing looking over these files. What am I hoping to find exactly? And, if I find something, who am I gonna call? WHISP-busters? Crone? I slam the folder shut and push the stack away from me. Maybe I am obsessed. Maybe my getting tossed off the case is a wake-up call, and the voice on the other end of the line is saying, 'Get over it, Harbinger. You did the best you could and now it's time to get on with your life. You owe it to yourself. You owe it to Ben and Lincoln.'

So, is this it? Am I giving it up? Just like that? I can't fool myself into thinking a part of me doesn't want to. It would be so much easier to pack these files up, put them in a box, head into the living room, plop down on the couch, and turn on a Sandra Bullock flick. I sit there searching my soul for a good long time, but I just can't do it. I'm not that person. Never was. I need to figure something out. I need more information. I need—

My cell phone rings. The display tells me it's Crone and my heart instantly turns to lead in my chest. I seriously consider not answering before I remember I practically begged him to keep me in the loop, and his calling probably means he wasn't nearly falling off his desk laughing at my expense this morning.

"Harbinger."

"It's time to celebrate, partner. We found her."

"Found who?"

"Seriously? The copycat. She even confessed."

CHAPTER 32

"A new company with a novel idea is making a name for itself in the porn industry. ShadowSexx makes films which depict WHISPs having sex. Founder, Hernando Smith, says no CGI is used in his films, but that lining up the actors' WHISPs has proved challenging."

HBO Special "The Future of Sex"

WHEN I GET OFF THE PHONE WITH CRONE, I HAVE NO idea what I've said to him. I'm not sure what I thought I'd feel when they caught the right-handed imposter, but it isn't this stewing impotence, this sense of uselessness and doubt. They'd caught the copycat. The case was all wrapped up with a nice neat bow and I didn't even get to be there for it. Except it wasn't. *Or was it?* No, screw that. I'm in way too deep to start questioning my sanity again. But now I don't even have Crone on my side. I'm all alone, or, at least, I will be until there's another murder while Chester and the copycat are incarcerated. Will the NYPD go chasing after another fictional cult member?

But I can't wait for that to happen. I can't see glossy photos of another mutilated victim just so I can be validated. *Think,*

Harbinger, think dammit. Pacing, along the path in my file-strewn office, I try to come up with some semblance of a plan. In order to stop the killing, I have to stop either Chester or Ray. To stop Ray, I need to know where she's going to strike, only Chester could have connections to places I don't even know about. I need to get the WHISP to come to a place I already know about. My mind tallies through locations and one sticks out. Chester's old apartment could work if I'm able to call in a favor.

Now I have a place in mind, I need to figure out a way to lure Chester's WHISP there or get Chester to send her there. To do that, I'm going to have to go see her and probably get her riled up again, and I need to do it sooner rather than later. While everyone at the precinct already knows I've been thrown off the case, I'm hoping Coppola didn't call Rikers and ban me from visitation with Chester. Probably, he didn't have time with the apprehension of the copycat and the solving of this big, public case. I check my watch. It's still just within visiting hours.

———

WHEN I SET UP THE INTERVIEW, THE RIKERS official wasn't thrilled about it, to say the least. More completely pissed off, actually, and after what happened at my last visit, I couldn't really blame him. I'd had to put the weight of the FBI, a weight I no longer wielded, behind the request to get him to acquiesce, but finally he gave in under the condition she and I be separated by bulletproof glass. A more personal atmosphere would've been better for what I had planned, but I had to take what I could get, at this point.

Sweat beads on my forehead as guards, maybe the same ones who'd yanked me from the room when Chester had attacked me, escort me to a different visitation room. This room is more the typical type portrayed on television with a half wall of bulletproof glass divided by partitions into semiprivate visitation cubicles. On each side of the glass is a counter and a telephone so the inmate on one side can communicate with the visitor on the other. I sit in the plastic chair in the cubicle the guards point me to at the far left of the room.

One guard peels away and exits, while the other takes up a station in front of the exit. While I wait for Chester, I wonder if the one guard has stayed only because I'd caused trouble on my last visit. After all, the shatterproof glass would prevent any inmate from getting through to this side of the room.

"Any chance I can get a little privacy here?"

The guard gives me a glare, eye twitching.

I point to the glass. "She can't get to me, and I have to ask her some sensitive questions."

He remains aloof.

"Please?"

His jaw tightens, and right before I think he's going to read me the riot act, he must decide he has better things to do.

"Fine. There's a panic button next to the phone if you need it. Otherwise, I'll be back in thirty minutes to collect you. This door will be locked. If you try to open it an alarm will sound. If you finish before your time is up, use the intercom next to the door to call a guard to let you out."

The guard then uses the intercom himself to call for someone to unlock the door, giving his name and badge number and then punching a code into the keypad. When the door buzzes and the guard opens it to exit, I call out to him.

"Thank you."

He doesn't answer me. When he's gone, the room seems more closed in and menacing. I've thought about what I'm going to say to Chester, and changed my mind half a dozen times. Even though I know Chester is behind Ray's actions, I can't go through with my plan to catch the WHISP without first calling Chester out and giving her a chance to stop killing. If what the woman at CAW said is true, separating Chester from her WHISP could cause her severe pain and damage her mentally even more than she already is. I can't have that on my soul, even if she is a cold-blooded killer, but once I've warned her, I've done my part and whatever happens afterwards is on her.

It isn't long before Chester, once again in wrist and ankle chains joined in front of her, shambles in accompanied by two guards. Neither is a guard from our previous visit. Once Chester is seated in the chair, one of the guards pushes her close enough to the counter so, even shackled, she can reach the phone while the other stands clear, hand on the Taser at his belt. When she's in position, both guards take up a position by the door. Chester leans forward and rests her elbows on the counter, then rests her head in her hands in a lazy gesture, though the chains linking her arms and legs must be uncomfortably tight. She stares at me like a cat. No, not a cat, a jaguar. Even in chains on the other side of a glass barrier, I am prey to her.

I keep my gaze focused on her face. This is the first time I've seen her since I figured out the truth about Ray, and more than ever I want to avoid looking at her WHISP. Picking up the phone, I try not to look rushed, but I don't have much time with her and I don't know if I'll ever get this opportunity again. Chester glances sidelong at the phone and her mouth spreads into a grin full of malice. She knows she could screw with me simply by not picking up the phone, keep me coming back and going through all this trouble just to have me sit here like an idiot. Fortunately, Chester also likes to talk. She waits only a few more minutes, staring at me with those predatory eyes before finally sighing and reaching for the phone.

"We've got to stop meeting like this, Detective. I mean that honestly, I'm not looking forward to another trip to the emergency room."

"You look fine to me, besides you're not in a threatening position today."

"Aren't I?"

I shake my head. "Not with this glass, not with those guards, not in this place, and not with me."

Her eyes narrow. "Oh?"

"Cut the act. I know everything. I know you haven't stopped killing, though I can't imagine it's much of a thrill when you can't be there. When you can't see it and hear it and get warm arterial blood splattered on your face. Really, I don't know why you're bothering."

Appraising me anew, Chester smiles. "Detective Harbinger, I am so proud of you. I never thought we'd get there with you. Bravo."

"Why still do it?"

She shrugs. "Habits are difficult to break sometimes."

"Hmm, maybe it's not you at all? Maybe Ray's just going off and doing it on her own now. Is that what you mean? It would make more sense seeing as how now you only get to hear about it secondhand on the news. Must be frustrating."

"You assume it's about the thrill. It's not. It's about power. It's about showing you I've beat you even though you put me in here. You're also assuming a...lack of connection."

I swallow. "You can't tell me you can see anything or hear anything through Ray." *Oh please God, tell me it isn't true.*

"Obviously not, but there are certain shared," she shivers with disconcerting pleasure, "impulses."

Bile splashes up into the back of my throat and I have to swallow hard.

Catching my reaction, Chester's smile turns condescending. "Still so much for you to learn, Detective."

"I know more than you think."

"Oh really? Such as?"

It's time to put it all out there, throw down the gauntlet and try to lure her into it. "I know you can't have Ray away from you for more than an hour at best. I know it puts a strain on you when she's away. I know she can only be sent to places she's familiar with, places you've spent a lot of time, and I know she can only hurt other people with WHISPs."

Chester raises her thin brows. "Very go—"

"—I also know something you might not. I know what you're doing is dangerous for you. The connection you have with her. It can hurt you. If Ray gets caught up in a strong magnetic field or her particles are dispersed somehow, not only will it be agonizing for you. It could seriously damage you. Permanently."

The irritation of me cutting her off fades into suspicion, but it quickly dissolves and Chester rolls her shoulders. "Hasn't happened yet. I think you're underestimating what's possible."

"Yeah? Why don't you show me then?"

"I wish I could"—her eyes trace over her shoulder and she sticks a thumb out toward the guards—"but now isn't the time."

"Fine, not now. Tomorrow night. At your old apartment." It's a clumsy and transparent attempt, but I'm running short on time even assuming the guard doesn't come back early just to be an ass.

Her eyes glitter. "Now why on earth would I do that, Detective?"

"To prove it to me. To flaunt your power. To have a chance to scare the crap out of me."

"Then why would *you*?"

Deliberately, I break eye contact. "Maybe to prove it to myself." I have to make her believe I'm questioning myself, my sanity, but I can't lay it on too thick. If she sees through the ruse, she won't send Ray because she knows I'm faking, and if she thinks I'm really having a breakdown, she might not come just to feed the flames of doubt. Clearing my throat, I straighten and find her eyes again. "Well?"

"I'll consider it. But if you aren't sincere in your motives, I'd hate to think of what it might mean to those around you."

"What do you mean by that?"

Chester's face brightens with malicious glee. "I read a very interesting article in the paper the other day. It was an editorial written by a Janet something? Anyways, she had very strong opinions about you with respect to your son and his WHISP."

My fingers grip the counter and my mouth goes dry. Janet Williams was the journalist who'd gotten wind of my WHISP phobia and written a scathing article about my bias in the case against Chester. Lincoln didn't share my last name, and didn't live with us, but it wouldn't have been too difficult for a professional journalist to figure out he was my son and he had a WHISP. "My son?"

"Mmm hmm, we worked in the same lab for a short time, but I'm sure you knew that."

"Are you threatening my son?"

"That's up to you."

Words gather in the back of my throat, but before I can speak again, the door behind me opens and the guard comes in.

"Time's up, Detective."

On the other side of the glass, Chester shrugs and hangs up the phone.

CHAPTER 33

"Just when you thought things couldn't get weirder in Japan, a new specialty clothing store is selling outfits for WHISPs. The store, roughly translated as 'Shadow Wear,' sells specially designed wire frames which hold up clothing so it looks like your WHISP is dressed. The frame can be swung to the side to allow the wearer to sit, and functions best when walking or standing."

The Daily Show, Comedy Central

IT ONLY TOOK CALLING IN A SMALL FAVOR TO GET ME into Chester's apartment. Fortunately, a snarl of legal issues has kept it empty since Chester was arrested. Some of the furniture is still there, but all of Chester's possessions have long since been removed. The place has a quiet air of neglect but, for me, also a cloud of horror. I visit each location where we found a piece of evidence: a bloodied shirt stuffed into a plastic bag, a pair of shoes with treads consistent with those found at two of the murder scenes, a clump of hair which turned out to be from Henry Hunt, and a scrap of fabric caught in the band of a broken watch, matched to the shirt of Grant Wilcox.

But there's no time to dwell in the past, and I'm not here for some kind of spiritual or emotional journey. I take out the video camera and set it up in the corner facing the couch. Then I pull out the item I bought from a less than squeaky clean pawn broker who'd given me information in the past in return for leniency on various transgressions. Never did I think I would be strapping one of these things on my back, but here I am. The device is heavy and its weight awkward despite shoulder straps and a waist strap. Taking a deep breath, I switch on the WHISP generator and listen to it hum and whine.

I've also purchased the optional heat shield pad, but the heat the device is generating is already starting to make me sweat. Resisting the urge to glance over my shoulder, I pull out the third item from my bag of tricks, which, in retrospect, should have been the second thing. It's supposed to be an EMP device, but for obvious reasons, I haven't tested it yet. I also can't resist sliding my gun out of its holster and laying it on the cushion next to me, for all the good it will do against a murderous cloud.

The trap is set, but I can't know whether it can possibly work and if it does, I can't know whether the EMP will work. If Chester is directing Ray, there's really no reason to think she'll decide to send her here, of all the other locations she could guide her. I can only hope no other places she's spent a lot of time in have a person with a WHISP unwarily crossing paths with Ray while I sit here watching the darkening skies. Since turning on the WHISP generator, and dubbing myself a target, my heart has been racing.

The medical examiner concluded the deaths of Chester's victims had been due to exsanguination, so theoretically, I would have some time to fight back. Also, I know, or at least think I know, what's coming, so I'm at an advantage over other victims who may never have understood what was happening to them. Still, I can't overlook the fact I'm using myself as bait for a serial killer, one whose handiwork has fueled my nightmares for the past year. My fingers trail across the top of the EMP. The slippery metal isn't nearly as comforting as the cool steel of my gun. And now comes the waiting.

———

MY ADRENALINE LONG SINCE EBBED, ONLY THE BURN of the WHISP generator and the ache it's founding in my back is keeping me from dozing. It's been close to five hours now and though I've drunk sparingly from my water bottle, I'm practically floating. This was probably a dumb idea, but it was the only one I had. Now I'm wondering if this prolonged exposure to the WHISP generator might be dangerous to my health, or worse, might trigger the development of a real WHISP. Then my cell phone rings, nearly causing me to piss myself. As I pull it from my pocket, images of cell phones shoved into carved up throats flood my mind, and violent shivers race up my spine.

It's Ben. No surprise there. In fact, I feel he showed incredible restraint by not calling until now. I click the ringer off and slip the phone back into my pocket. I was out with Kristina at a bar, and I didn't hear my phone ring. An easy lie. I'm just relaxing back into the couch when my phone rings again and, jolted, I bite my tongue. When I yank the phone from my pocket, I'm seeing red and tasting blood. I check the settings and find the phone thinks the ringer is off, yet the chimes are still echoing through the vacant apartment. I turn the ringer on and then off again and the ringing stops.

Spooked now, I scan the dim room illuminated solely by my cell phone and by the glow of my faux WHISP. I spot the WHISP in the window and knock the EMP to the floor, grabbing my gun instead through force of habit. This turns out to be a good thing because, a moment later, I grasp that I'm staring at the reflection of my faux WHISP.

"Dammit!" Fear and anger turn to giddiness. "You scared me."

The reflection of the hologram lowers its hands as I lower my gun. I'm caught in morbid fascination and raise my arms slowly back up into firing position, then back down again, then holster my Glock and swing my arms around in circles. The slightly blue-tinged, cloudy shadow mimes me. I wave at it and as it waves back. The punch-drunk mirth is replaced by revulsion. Striding over to the window, I drop the blinds and find my hands are shaking. The discomfort in my bladder has now turned to pain. It's a few minutes after three a.m. and I don't know how much longer I can stay here with this thing on my back. I won't be able to defend myself if I'm completely exhausted, and if I don't return home soon or at least call Ben, he might call the precinct.

I pull out the phone and start to text Ben when it rings again, but this time with an unfamiliar ringtone. "What the fuck?"

The screen reads, "Ben Calling," so I breathe in and answer.

"Sorry, Babe, I'm out with Kristina and we just lost track of time. I didn't hear the ringer before."

Angry static hisses and buzzes through the phone's speaker.

"Ben? Ben can you hear me?"

The beep, beep, beep of a lost call sounds, so I wait a few moments for Ben to call back, but he doesn't.

"Fuck."

I begin the text anew, but my phone kicks me out of the texting app before I can finish. I enter the app again and start typing but it kicks me out again. Gripped with annoyance, I turn off the phone intending to turn it back on again. It's then a sensation of cold, empty wrongness manifests deep in my gut.

I'm turning to collect the EMP from the floor when something crashes into the back of my head and sends me sprawling. Bright flashes of color burst like fireworks across the back of my eyes, and the gentle hum of the WHISP generator increases steadily until it's a deafening whine. Searing heat rages across my back as I struggle up onto my hands and knees. At first, I think the WHISP device has exploded, but then I catch sight of a blurry cloud in front of me. Ray. I lunge forward toward the EMP on the floor, but Ray charges and I'm being tugged backwards, the straps of the WHISP generator biting into my shoulders.

Falling back, I catch a glimpse of the video camera whizzing toward me. It impacts my skull with an audible crack and white, blinding pain explodes in my head. The whining of the WHISP generator reaches a crescendo then changes to a screech, which peaks and then goes silent. I'm blinking, but I only see blackness overlaid with the after images of colorful sparks. I'm tumbling then, not physically but mentally, vaguely aware of the throbbing in my head, burning of my back, and warmth spreading down my thighs.

CHAPTER 34

"I find bright sunny days and wearing grey or other dark colors minimizes WHISP visibility."

Blog: Learning to Live With a WHISP

"Sʏʟᴠʏ, ʙᴀʙʏ?"

Ben's voice carries to me over various beeps and whirrs. I'm lying on a hard, cold bed with sheets that scratch at the backs of my bare legs. Blackness gradually dissolves into pale light and the stink of disinfectant invades my nose. In a flood of memory, I know exactly where I am and how I got here.

"The camera…" my voice is hardly a rasp, the inside of my mouth tacky and dry. "Water."

Someone's hand squeezes mine, then I feel a straw poking at my parched lips. I take one minute sip after another until my tongue doesn't feel like beef jerky and I can swallow without pain.

"I'm here, babe."

I blink until my eyes finally open, but at first all I see is yellow light. "Did you get the camera?"

"Shhh, it's okay. Everything's okay now."

I try to shake my head, but more just rock it back and forth. Nothing is okay. Slowly, Ben's face emerges from the blur of light.

"Did you see it?"

He frowns. "See what?"

"On the camera, the WHISP."

His frown deepens and he opens his mouth, then closes it and clears his throat. "Let's not talk about it now."

My languid unconsciousness is falling away rapidly, an anxious mania replacing it as I try to sit up. "No, no. The WHISP, I caught it on camera, it attacked me."

Ben's hands are on my shoulders. "Easy, easy. Someone did attack you. Crone is looking into the possibility that the copycat had accomplices—"

"No! It was—"

A nurse enters the room, her face marked by lines of unhappy concern. With her appearance, I'm acutely aware of things like restraints and sedation. I freeze and stay quiet, avoiding her gaze.

"Is everything all right in here?"

I catch Ben's eye with mine and plead with him silently. He's struggling, maybe trying to decide whether I'm lucid or not.

"Yeah, she, ah, just woke up and she...she didn't know where she was, but she's okay now."

"I'm okay now."

The nurse gives Ben a hard look. "All right. I'm just outside the door if you need me."

"Thank you."

When she's gone, he stares down at me and takes my hand between both of his. For a while he just runs his thumb gently back and forth over the top of my hand while I repress my exasperation, so I won't shout the next time I open my mouth. Finally, he says, "What were you doing there?"

"Didn't you watch the video?"

His eyes are blank. "Yes. I saw you activate a WHISP generator and sit on a couch with your gun out."

A pain begins in my chest and works its way into my throat. I can't believe this is happening. "You didn't see me get attacked?"

"No." Wrinkles appear along his forehead like waves on a smooth surface of water. "After you ignored my phone calls, all it recorded was static."

"Static?"

He nods.

I close my eyes. "I am so stupid." Why on earth did I think a digital camera was going to work in the presence of an aggressive, untethered WHISP? Tears squeeze out under my eyelids and I draw in a sharp breath which is too much like a sob.

"Listen, never mind, I don't care, it doesn't matter. What matters is you're okay...and that you...you just stop, whatever this is."

I pull my hand from his and wipe the tears away. "How long have I been unconscious? How bad were my injuries?" In my mind, I'm piecing together input from my body: no cracked ribs, no broken bones, but head trauma and my back...

"What does it matter? Pretty bad. You've been out about twelve hours, have a concussion and second degree burns on your back." Ben runs his hand through his hair like he wants to tear hunks of it out. "Sylvy, please, just relax and rest. Please just, just stop. Just for a minute think about someone other than yourself. I know you feel like you're the only one who can save the world from killers and...and bad things, but you've put in your time. The NYPD even knew it, they kicked you off the case. Now you have to realize it. Let it go. Whatever you're holding onto, let it go. Please. For me, for your family, for your son."

His words are a million shards of ice piercing my heart. Anger, nausea, guilt, shame, stubbornness, and emotions I don't even have a name for are fighting for control of my head and my gut. I can delude myself I'm on this vigilante quest only to save lives, and no one else will accept the truth, but right now all I'm doing is almost getting myself killed and proving to others I'm crazy. And I'm destroying my marriage...again. I'm alone and suffocating in a dark, horrible place and the walls are collapsing all around me, burying me. If I let him, Ben can pull me out, he's done it before, but only if I let him.

"I...I'm an ass. A self-righteous ass with delusions of grandeur. I know you don't understand, but I did what I did because I thought it would save lives and I didn't think there was another way. I'm sorry."

Ben crushes me in a hug. The bandages on my back rip away and I bite my lip to keep from crying out.

"I know you did, baby, I know."

The tears are flowing freely now, and my head is pounding, but it feels good. No, not exactly good, but good like when you worry a loose baby tooth right before it falls out. "Did you call Lincoln? I don't want him to see me like this."

"I did, but his phone just went to voice mail. He must be in the lab. He said he was going to be working on a new project using the particle accelerator and he was pretty excited about it."

Something like an itch is breaking through the ache in my brain. I lean back. "I thought the particle accelerator was in Lincoln's old lab, the one he worked in when he started grad school."

"It is. That's actually why he's been allowed to use it, because he worked in the lab before."

Suddenly the itch becomes a fire and a thought slams home.

No. Oh, please no. Rachel Chester was a physics student at NYU. She worked in Lincoln's old lab, and she even knew him. Lincoln had told me so shortly after she was arrested. She'd spent a lot of time in the lab. It was her home away from home.

"Oh no."

CHAPTER 35

"We aren't talking about hate. We're talking about preservation of the human race."

Excerpt: CAW manifesto

I'M OUT OF THE BED BEFORE I EVEN KNOW WHAT I'M doing. The I.V. stand clatters to the floor as the tubes attached to my arm pull taut. My bare feet slip backwards on the smooth tile, and when I realize the I.V. line is holding me back, I claw at the tape holding the needle in my arm to free myself. As the needle slides out of my vein, Ben grabs me from behind.

"Syvly! What are you doing?"

The nurse flies into the room before I can answer, sees us grappling and runs back out again shouting, "I need help in here!"

I have no time. I drop to my knees and spin to face my husband. "Ben, please, you have to listen to me. Lincoln's in danger. We have to go find him. We have to get him out of the lab right now. Please. God, Ben, please. I know you think I'm crazy, but the—my attacker is going after Lincoln. I know it!"

His mouth slightly open, his eyes wide, his face awash in

shock and horror, I'm sure Ben's going to grab me again and help hold me down when they come to sedate me, but then something changes. He closes his mouth and his cheek twitches. His eyes flick to his coat hanging on a hook near the door. Seizing it, he ducks down and scoops me up, throwing the coat around my shoulders. "Here, put this on."

I'm so grateful I want to fall into his embrace, but instead I thread my arms into the armholes as he half-carries me into the hallway. We almost make it around the corner before someone calls out behind us.

"Hey! Hey you!"

With his arm under my shoulder, Ben and I break into a flat run, turn the corner, and barrel through a set of double doors. Since I have no idea what part of the hospital we're in, I let him guide me down the hall and around another corner. At the end of this hallway, I spot elevators and a stairwell and surge toward them, but he drags me off my feet and abruptly I'm in a dark room. The automatic overhead lights flicker on and I find we're crouching in a bathroom. Ben has his ear to the door, but even I can hear the tromping of feet as they pass.

Cracking the door, he peers out and then we're up and hurrying away from the elevators. We pass through another set of double doors with a sign declaring imaging to be on the other side. We walk quickly, but try not to draw attention as we wind through more corridors with Ben verifying our route every time we pass a map on the wall. When we come upon an unoccupied wheelchair, he sits me in it. I want to argue with him, but I'm too busy suppressing dry heaves to speak.

We reach another bank of elevators and he presses the button then calmly wheels me into the elevator when it arrives. Within the elevator are two doctors, one a tall, black woman and the other a thick-set Asian man, discussing some reality show, and a janitor with a bucket and mop. Neither the doctors nor the janitor do more than glance at us when we first get on, still, my fingers grip the handles of the wheelchair with white knuckles. We were on the sixth floor and the elevator stops at the fifth to let the doctors off then at the third to let the janitor off. Every time the doors open, I expect to see stern-faced orderlies with straightjackets and large syringes, but only an elderly woman with a cane greets us on the third floor and she doesn't get on because she says she needs to go up.

When it's only the two of us on the elevator, I expect Ben to start grilling me, yet he remains silent, staring at the digital display for the floor numbers. Then we're at ground level and he's rolling me toward signs for the parking garage. My heart flutters in my chest like a caged bird as I picture a blockade of hospital security that never materializes. Eventually, we are out in the structure and I slump in the wheelchair, resting my head on my arm. Gnawing, sickly hunger rakes at my stomach and the world spins behind my closed eyelids. The motion stops and I look up to see my car hastily parked and close to taking up two spots.

Ben is at my elbow and helping me to stand. Again, I want to tell him I don't need his help, but I do, and the lie would only wind up with me on the ground. He eases me into the passenger side then dives into the driver's seat and starts the car almost simultaneously, throwing it into reverse and backing out. I pop open the glove box and reach inside, rummaging until my fingers close around the emergency candy bar I have stashed there. With shaking fingers and a groaning stomach, I peel back the wrapper and shove fully half of the bar into my mouth. It's too big a bite to chew comfortably, but I manage to get it down without choking despite Ben taking the turns of the parking structure at breakneck speeds.

He slows as we reach the exit, but just long enough to slide his credit card through the unmanned pay station kiosk. Moments later, we're peeling out onto the street and I'm hanging onto the arm rests for dear life. When the car stops fishtailing, Ben speaks without taking his eyes off the road.

"Tell me."

Knowing he's not really going to believe me, but hoping that he continues driving toward Lincoln anyway, I swallow the rest of the candy bar and cough roughly as a peanut chunk goes down the wrong pipe. Finally, able to speak, I lay it all out.

"It's complicated, but like I said before, I think Chester is somehow using Ray to murder people. It seems like she can do it anywhere if she's there, which is how she got blood on her clothes, but while she's stuck in prison, she can only send Ray to places she's lived or spent extensive periods of time, and she can only murder people with Ray if they have a WHISP. She worked in Lincoln's old lab for almost a year...and he has a WHISP."

Ben's face is smooth and blank. "She can't know he has a WHISP."

I shake my head. "It was in the paper, in the article by that horrible reporter calling me a WHISP bigot."

As a flash of remembrance brightens his eyes, Ben licks his lips. I don't know what it was, but something I've said has started the gears of belief spinning in his head.

"All of her victims had a WHISP?"

"Yes." He knows this, but I can see he needs to hear it again.

Now he's chewing on the bottom of his lip and mumbling to himself. I recognize a smattering of physics terms in the mix. We turn a corner and Ben slams on the breaks, barely avoiding rear-ending a Chevy Impala. All the traffic ahead is at a dead stop.

"Dammit!"

For a fleeting instant, I fight the impulse to jump out of the car and start running, but we're still at least two miles away and I'm in no condition. Also, my feet are bare and I'm wearing nothing but a hospital gown and a coat. Ben is scanning the traffic, his face a contortion of wild frustration.

"Sylvy, grab my phone. It's in my coat pocket."

Digging my hands into the coat, I locate the phone and turn it on. "Got it."

"Find me a way around this fucking mess."

The traffic has inched forward since we stopped, but there's no obvious cause for the backup, so no way to know how long it will last. Unlocking the phone, I bring up the map. The app has helpfully indicated there is an accident ahead of us.

"There's an accident on 29th near 3rd, take 2nd if you can."

But I can see Ben has other ideas. He's spotted an alley on our left and his hand is poised over the switches that activate the car's lights and siren. This could cost me my pension.

"Do it."

CHAPTER 36

"These aren't tech-junkies we're talking about, these are everyday people: mothers, teachers, sons, daughters, doctors. Normal people manifesting WHISPs every day."

Interview: Dr. Darshana Grover, The Center for WHISP Wellness and Research

WITH LIGHTS FLASHING AND SIREN BLARING, WE careen over the curb and onto the sidewalk, something I'd never done before as a police officer. It's liberating and terrifying at the same time as pedestrians stop in their tracks to avoid coming into our path. My eyes dart back and forth, watching for bicyclists, nuns, and runaway strollers, but the way to the alley is blissfully open. Ben clears the entrance and begins weaving to avoid dumpsters and piles of cardboard boxes that might house the homeless.

"Look out!"

A man with ear buds jammed in his ears is taking out the trash from the back of a restaurant and steps into our path before seeing us. Ben jerks the steering wheel and takes out the blue plastic trashcan but misses the man and I fit myself back into my skin. Then we're coming to the end and he's pumping the brakes so we don't shoot out into the stream of traffic. Praying people hear the sirens, I brace against the dashboard as Ben steers the car out of the alley, over the curb, and back onto the street then floors it again. Normally, he's conservative on the roads, so I'm dazed and wondering where he's been hiding this inner NASCAR driver.

"Hold on!"

Leaving screeching tires and honking horns behind us, Ben makes a left turn from the right lane at a yellow light. The adrenaline rush twitches the corners of my lips, but then I focus. I have to believe we're going to get there in time, but how can we protect Lincoln from Ray?

"What would a particle accelerator do to a WHISP?"

Teeth clenched and bared, Ben is threading the needle between two buses. "What?"

"WHISP, particle accelerator, what would happen?"

"It would fly apart...but you'd have a tough time getting it in there. The walls are meant to keep super accelerated particles in, so you'd need it to go through an open access panel."

My mind is whirling through possibilities, but none strike me as valid. We need something like a reverse grenade, something we could toss into the particle accelerator which would go off and suck the WHISP in after it. Maybe some kind of remote electromagnet? But then I remember Lila Grant's chilling words about the pain tearing a person's WHISP away from them causes. It would have to be something we could shield Lincoln's WHISP from. I need to figure this out with Ben, I need time, but we're nearly there and something is going on.

For one agonizing span of breath, I think we're too late, that the commotion ahead of us has been caused by the mob of police cars and ambulances responding to Lincoln's attack. Everything goes silent except the beating of my heart, loud and frantic in my ears, then I see the scene for what it is. Students are gathered in the street blocking traffic and the police cars are for patrolmen helping to contain the demonstration. In the chaos, one sign, white with red paint, stands out from the others. On it are the words, 'WHISP RIGHTS.' *Right now? Seriously?*

"Fuck!"

Ben slams on the brakes again, and only the locking of my seatbelt prevents my limp body from impacting the dashboard. Recovering quickly, I jab at the belt release and cinch Ben's coat tight.

"There's no way around, we have to get out."

Abandoning the car, we head toward the crowd. Ben is helping me over a barricade when an arm grips my shoulder and spins me around.

"Whoa, hey ma'am, are you okay? Detective Harbinger?"

Schmitty's wide eyes wander from the bandages around my head to my bare feet on the cold cement. His lips move but no words come out.

"We have to get through to the physics lab."

Seeing a stern-faced Ben, Schmitty releases my arm. "Is there trouble?"

Schmitty might be able to help us, but there's no time for explanations. "No, not—"

"It's fine. We'll make it ourselves."

Ben vaults the barrier and I grip his arm for support. Together, we leave a slack jawed Schmitty and press into the throng of chanting students. Feeling like a sailor in the middle of a hurricane, I cling to Ben's arm like a life raft as we get bumped and jostled. My bare foot gets stomped on and I almost go down, but Ben's arms are around me and we're on the move again. He gets clipped by an enthusiastic sign waver and I see a crescent of blood on his cheek. The sign wielder gets in front of

Ben stammering an apology, and he knocks the boy aside with his shoulder to clear the way.

I'm shocked at the size of the protest and can't see the edges of it. All I can see are bodies and signs and angry faces...and WHISPs. Once I spot one of them, they are impossible not to see mixed in among the other students, and my pulse reaches a frantic staccato as the familiar strangling fear of my phobia takes hold. Ben must feel me tense and slow because he turns to me.

"What is it?"

"They're everywhere..."

He tugs at my arm, but my legs are trembling and refuse to carry me forward. So many shadowy clouds; they're closing in around me. Ben takes my face in his hands.

"Sylvy, we have got to move. We've got to get to Lincoln."

Lincoln, my poor neglected boy who must know I can barely stand to be in the same room with him. I have to get to him. I have to save him. I can do this. I can do this for Lincoln. I owe him this.

Nodding, I close my eyes and allow Ben to drag me forward, but our progress is too slow. I open my eyes again and am assaulted once more by the sight of the WHISPs in the crowd, but I steel myself. They can't hurt me, not this time.

Then, without any forewarning, we're through and I can see the lab building. My feet feel like I've been treading on broken glass, but I keep pace with Ben as we hurl up the steps and to the door. He grabs the handle, and the door vibrates violently but doesn't open. Catching my breath, I point to a card reader on the adjacent wall with a glowing red light. "It's locked."

"Fuck!"

He smacks a hand against the glass, and casts around as if looking for something to smash the glass, but I'm already heading back down the stairs.

"Where are you going?"

"That's safety glass, we need to find another way in!"

Not waiting for Ben, I leap a short stone wall and head around the side of the building. There aren't any convenient low windows and any I might be able to reach by climbing are safety windows that don't open far enough for someone to climb in, so I keep going. Ben catches up and tries another door, but it's also locked with a card reader. Rounding the back of the building, I skid to a stop as I spot a service door without a card reader. This one is made of metal and has a simple dead-bolt. After he finds this door locked as well, Ben sprints away.

"Wait! I can pick this one."

"With what?"

A list of lock picking tools flash through my mind: a nail file, nail scissors, a hairpin, a paperclip, a lightbulb filament, the spring from a pen...

"A pen!"

I fumble through Ben's coat and come up with a ball point pen. Disassembling it, I retrieve the spring, straighten it, and then twist it into the proper shape. He dances impatiently from one foot to the other while I insert the spring into the lock. I steady my shaking fingers so I can feel the delicate mechanism inside and with a few deft motions the tumblers give way, but the spring is too flimsy to turn the lock.

"Get the clip off the pen and use it to turn the deadbolt."

When Ben sticks the clip from the pen into the lock, the deadbolt turns. Dropping the clip, he grips the handle, and as I straighten, the door swings open.

CHAPTER 37

"Legislative reforms are never a speedy proposal, but never before has Congress faced such a fraught and complicated issue as WHISP rights."

Harney Glutz, (R) Delaware

I'M HOLDING MY BREATH, BUT LET IT OUT WHEN NO alarms go off. The door opens into a stark stairwell, but the lab is in the basement and there are no stairs leading down here.

"Dammit!"

"We'll have to go up and find another stairwell."

Nodding, I follow Ben up the steps while I'm trying to orient myself with where we are in the building. I'd been to the lab a few times to take Lincoln out to lunch, but it's been a while. At the landing, we exit into a hallway lined with labs and offices. Sprinting down the hall, we startle a student coming out of one of the labs, and he drops the binder he's carrying, which spews papers in a wide arch around him. "Hey!"

We don't slow for an apology. Luckily, the building is otherwise deserted, thanks to the upcoming long weekend. At a fork, we head right, which I think is toward the front of the building, and make it down a similar hallway to a second stairwell that looks less neglected. Taking the stairs two at a time, I slip and narrowly avoid a nasty tumble by clutching the handrail at the last moment.

Vertigo slows my pace, but then I see the stairs continue down past the ground floor and I get another surge of adrenaline. Ahead of me, Ben is already through the landing door and I push myself to catch up to him.

He slows to look at the numbers next to the doors but then runs a hand over his slick forehead and through his hair, wetting it and causing it to stick up. "Dammit, I don't remember what number it is!"

"It's 27A. Go!"

My side is ready to explode and the pain in my feet is making my eyes water, but we're steps away from the lab now so I'm right on Ben's heels as he lunges forward around a corner.

"There!"

He reaches the door first and yanks it open. My heart is beating so hard my ribs are beginning to ache. Oh, please lord, please let Lincoln be okay. Ben takes a step inside and then all the color drains from his face. He looks to me and puts a hand up, but I'm already shoving past him into the chaos. Several instruments are sparking and smoking, there's a small fire in front of one of the outlets, and the fluorescent lights overhead flicker wildly, causing a strobe effect. It takes a moment for my eyes to adjust enough for me to take in the details, but then I see it. In the center of the room are the remains of a person, their blood splattering the nearby benches and equipment, pooling under the entrails strewn across the floor. The smell slaps me in the face: iron and viscera.

"NO!"

Lurching forward, I skid on blood and land on my knees next to the head of the body in a pool of gore. I'm shaking all over and I have to rub my eyes to clear them, and then again after they focus, when I think they're lying to me. This close, I can see the hair of the victim is long and blond. I let out a strangled cry as relief and horror permeate my insides.

"It's not—"

I see the instrument maybe a second before it strikes my face just below my right eye. There's a wet crack when it hits, and I'm momentarily blinded as pain shoots into my eye.

"Sylvy!" Ben's voice is pitched with anguish and I can sense him, more than see him, coming toward me.

"Don't..."

But it's too late. Now that he's fully inside the lab, one of the fluorescent lights shatters and rains glass down on him until the whole fixture crashes down on his head.

"Ben!"

My eyes dart around the room as I crawl through the slick blood to Ben's prone form. When I arrive and touch his face he stirs.

"Wha happen...?"

"It's the WHISP, it's still here."

"Lincoln..." Ben's voice is lost in a sob.

"No, no, it wasn't him. I don't see him. He must be in with the accelerator, and if Ray's still here, it must mean he's protected. Come on, we have to get to him before he comes out."

As I help Ben out from under the light, I see blood trickling from his head down the side of his face, and his clumsy movements are signs of a concussion. I get him on his feet and we crouch as we run toward the far end of the lab. There, a door is marked with a radiation symbol and a red triangle with the word danger inscribed in the middle in white. Halfway to the door, a centrifuge starts up and speeds faster and faster, wobbling alarmingly. Ben's arm slides around my waist. "Look out!"

He dives forward, taking me with him. The centrifuge launches off the lab bench and flies through the air landing just a few feet from us. It gouges a craterous hole as it embeds itself deep in the floor, discharging shrapnel and chunks of tile and concrete as it sparks and spins. Debris hits my leg and I scream as it tears through my flesh. Then Ben is hauling me up again and he slams us into the door to the accelerator. I'm standing on one shredded foot and I think that my leg is going to give out, but then we're through the door and I topple over, taking him with me. He rams the door shut with his foot and a glint of metal catches my eye. A piece of shrapnel as big as a pair of scissors is sticking out of his leg just above the knee and blood is soaking his pant leg. Ben's cheeks are flushed from exertion, but the rest of his face has gone ghostly white save the parts smeared with blood.

"Take off your belt."

He blinks at me then reaches down and gropes the buckle for a few seconds without any progress. Knocking his hands away, I undo the belt and pull it free from around his waist, then cinch it tight around his leg. He winces and groans. My own leg is throbbing, but a cursory glance tells me that it isn't a serious blood loss concern like Ben's leg. We're in a quite chamber now with white radiation suits hanging on pegs along the wall. The cacophony of the lab on the other side of the door is completely dampened by its thickness. There are two doors leading from the chamber, one with a sign reading 'observation room,' and one with a slew of warning signs. The door without the warning signs has a square of glass in it, but the other door does not. All is quiet here and the lights are steady.

"Can you stand?"

Ben's lips smile, but his eyes are dull. "I don't think so."

I help him into a more comfortable position, his face contorting with pain until he's propped up against the wall under the suits.

"It really wasn't Lincoln?"

I shake my head. "The body had blonde hair...I think it was a woman."

Ben glances up at the door to the lab. "I think I believe you now."

The laugh that ripples out of my throat like a bark is rough and scratchy and rides the fine line of hysteria. "Took you long enough."

When he looks at me, his ghost of a smile fades. "Sylvy, I'm so—"

"Stop. I know. I sounded insane."

He swallows and inclines his head toward the observation room door.

"Go. Go make sure Lincoln's safe."

I nod, then kiss him, ignoring the taste of blood on his lips and the flash of agony it elicits in my cheek.

"Mom? Dad?"

I turn and see Lincoln standing in the observation room doorway, a dislodged earbud dangling from one ear. "What's going on?"

CHAPTER 38

"Your love is like a shadow, like a WHISP of my heart. I can walk right through it, as it tears me apart."

WHISPs of Love by Death Nevermore

"OH LINCOLN, THANK GOD!"

I stand up, limp to him and throw my arms around his neck. I hug with all my waning strength. Lincoln returns the embrace but only with one tentative arm.

"What the hell happened to you two?"

Letting him go, I look back toward Ben then to Lincoln. "Is there a phone in the observation room?"

"No, why? Jesus, Mom, are you going to tell me what happened?" He looks past me. "Dad?"

"It's...a long story, but help me up. We have to get out of here."

Lincoln brushes past me and I stiffen as his WHISP passes close enough to touch, but I can't freeze up now.

"Ben, we can't get out that way. It'll be waiting for us, for *Lincoln*."

"Lincoln, who else was working here with you in the lab?"

Lincoln is trying to hoist Ben under one arm, so I take Ben's other arm. The observation room might at least be warmer than this chamber, and I have an irrational fear Ray can hear us or sense our thoughts through the door to the lab.

"Anna's in the lab. She's from Poland. Didn't you see her when you came in?"

My eyes find Ben's. "Does she have blonde hair?"

"Yeah, why?"

"I'm sorry, Lincoln. She's dead."

"What!"

"I'll explain everything, I promise, just help me get your dad into the observation room."

Lincoln and I have Ben up and are inching toward the other room with him. Ben's dead weight on my shoulders is concerning me. He's weak and the belt will only slow the blood loss. If I have Lincoln help me tighten it, Ben could lose his leg, but if he continues to lose blood, it won't be a problem anymore. He needs medical attention and soon. We get him into the observation room and I hobble back to grab two of the radiation suits off the wall, one to elevate Ben's leg after we lay him down and one to prop under his head.

"I'm going to go get help."

Lincoln strides out of the observation room and I have to lunge through his WHISP to grab his shoulder.

"No!"

"You can't," Ben's voice is strained.

Lincoln spins around to face me. "Why not?"

"There's someone out there who wants to kill you."

"Who?"

"Rachel Chester."

Darkness and disbelief spread across Lincoln's face. "This is insane. Rachel Chester's in prison."

"She uses her WHISP to kill people. It's how she kept killing from prison."

Lincoln grabs my upper arms and sits me down in a chair. "Mom, it was a copycat. They caught her. It was all over the news." Pity fills his voice, "You have to face reality."

He turns to leave again.

"It's true, Lincoln. I didn't believe your mother either, at first, but it's true. Chester's WHISP is out there and it almost killed us. It killed Anna, but it's here for you."

As I kneel next to Ben, I see the resolve in Lincoln's eyes falter.

"Dad, you can't really believe that. It doesn't make any sense."

"But it does. WHISPs are made of particles, radiation is made of particles..."—he takes a shaking breath—"that can hurt people."

Lincoln looks exactly like Ben when he's scrutinizing information in his head. I envision calculations on the back of his retinas. His brow furrows and the corners of his mouth turn down. "Wait, wait, wait, are you saying Chester killed all of her victims using her WHISP?"

So thankful Lincoln is finally convinced enough not to try to enter the lab, I nod so enthusiastically, my vision starts to swim. "Yes."

"Then why didn't she kill you two like...like she killed the others?"

"WHISPs can only interact directly with people who also have WHISPs, because...oh something to do with them being more open or susceptible to the particles."

"Then how did it hurt you guys?"

"It can act like a poltergeist on things with magnetic fields, anything electrical..." I'm about to wax poetic about the abilities of WHISPs and how I think Chester's is particularly strong because of her psychotic tendencies when Ben coughs. It's a long, rattling cough and it jars me back to the reality of the situation.

"Listen, the only way we can get your dad out of here is if we can kill or disintegrate—"

"Disperse." Ben coughs again.

"—disperse it. Your dad said the particle accelerator could do that, but we need something to draw it into the chamber. I was thinking a strong electromagnet might do it, but..."

"But what?"

"But it risks sucking your WHISP into the chamber, too."

"So what?"

"So...someone told me it's painful, really painful and...the person might not be right again afterwards." My voice catches. I want to reach out and touch Lincoln's face, but don't want to experience the pain of him possibly flinching away from me, so I'm still.

"Oh."

"But there must be another way to draw it in, maybe..." Then it hits me. "Lincoln, what would happen to a person in the accelerator?"

"In the path of the beam? A very fine beam of radiation would shoot through them and they'd probably die...well, maybe die. There was this Russian scientist, Anatoli Bugorski, he was hit in the head with the beam and lived. Never even showed signs of radiation poisoning. Everyone who works with particle accelerators has heard of him. But no one would ever be in there when it's operating. Usually it's a super-cooled vacuum. Why?" His banter slows from talking about something which interests and excites him to sluggish suspicion. "You're not thinking..."

"Does it have to be a vacuum? And what about the temperature? Can you leave it at room temperature?"

"Mom, I don't know what you're—"

"I could lure it in there and stay out of the beam. If I'm wearing a suit and it's not cold or a vacuum, I should be fine."

"No, no, there's got to be some other way—"

I glance down at Ben. He's still conscious, but his eyes are fluttering and the fact he hasn't responded to my plan is a very bad sign.

"Listen to me. Your father is going into shock, there might be another way to do this, but I don't know what it is and there's no time. You can't go in there with your WHISP, but I can. You and your dad will stay in here. I think the shielding of the door will protect you from Chester's WHISP. I'll get on a suit and open the lab door and try to draw it in. I assume you can open and close the access door to the tube from here."

Lincoln is shaking his head. "I can, but...but how will you even know the WHISP is in there with you?"

"Give me your cell phone."

"It doesn't get a signal in here, it's not going to get one in the tube. What are you going to do, dial 911 and throw it out into the lab?"

"No, no, the WHISP will probably just disable it out there. No, I need it to track the WHISP. It should malfunction if it's close, and if not then..."—I spot an emergency flashlight on the wall and rush over to grab it—"then I'll use this. I should be able to see Ray in oblique light even if she's kinda spread out."

He hands me the phone, but his hands are shaking. "Mom, I don't know..."

"Please, Lincoln, please just get it ready. You'll be able to see me, right? There're cameras?"

He nods. "Once you climb into the tube, I'll see you. Get down on the floor as low as you can right next to the wall. Flat. And when you see it in there, give me a signal and I'll...I'll close the hatch and start the accelerator."

"I'll give you a thumbs up, okay?"

Lincoln nods again. "There's a code, to open the outer door: thirty-six, sixty-eight."

"Thirty-six, sixty-eight." I smile at him. "This is going to work."

Then I kneel next to Ben. "Honey?" He stirs and his eyes focus on me. "Lincoln and I have a plan. We're going to get us out of here. I just need you to hang on for me, okay? Will you stay with us?"

Ben tilts his chin down a fraction of an inch. "I promise."

I kiss him again, and this time his lips taste of the salt from my tears instead of iron. Then I stand and face Lincoln, but before I can say anything, he grapples me in a hug.

"I love you, Mom."

My heart skips at the force of his hug. "I know. I love you, too." I want to stay in this moment, the first real hug Lincoln and I have shared in years, but there isn't time. Pulling away, I wipe at my tears and steady myself. "Get the machine ready, and whatever you do, don't open this door until it's done, okay?"

"Okay."

Turning, I take a deep breath and walk out into the entry chamber, closing the door behind me.

CHAPTER 39

"The New York Times is heralding the latest rural co-op craze as a return to the sixties, but electricity-free housing communities are big business these days. Also exploding are agricultural, organic, and environmental industries as well as, shockingly, the breeding of carrier pigeons."

CBS Special: The New Technophobia

ONCE OUTSIDE, I TAKE OFF BEN'S COAT TO MAKE IT easier to get into a radiation suit. My feet, leg, back, head, and swelling cheekbone are all vying for my attention, but I ignore them as I step into the white plastic. Before I slip my hands into the sleeves and thick gloves, I unlock Lincoln's phone, the first two numbers from his high school locker combination, and open the music app. I'd planned to just select the very first song, just something to listen for any disruption, but when a playlist comes up I spot *Bolero* near the bottom. It's as good as any song and long enough there should be less chance of the music dying out when I still need it. Hitting play, I bump the volume up as loud as it will go. As I resume donning the suit, I listen to the first soft beats of drum and don't allow myself any time to dwell on the profoundly stupid thing I'm about to do. Ben's dying, there's no time for weighing pros and cons, no time to consider the wide, ragged flaws in my plan. In fact, it may already be too late, he may have lost too much blood, but I can still save my son.

Once the suit's on, it's bulky yet gives little protection from the chill of this part of the lab. As the clear mask immediately begins to fog, I realize I'm breathing too fast through my mouth, so I take a deep breath in through my nose and then let it out through my mouth. Palming Lincoln's cell phone in one gloved hand and the flashlight in the other, I face the door to the lab. Even though it seems there isn't much for Chester's WHISP to harm me with in this corridor, my heart rockets as I reach forward and take the handle. "Here we go."

I turn the handle and throw the door wide. Outside, the lab is dark save for residual sparking and flames coming from damaged machines, and I want to believe the WHISP may have gone. Maybe a guard went to check on Chester or bring her a meal and she had to call Ray back. However unlikely, the scenario is still possible, yet my gut is telling me a different story. I turn the flashlight on and swing it up, holding it and the phone as I would my pistol if entering an un-cleared, dimly lit scene. The first soft strains of music are intensifying as the beam illuminates the gloom of the lab. I play the light back and forth almost in time with the music, and, at first, I see nothing but destruction and carnage.

The weaponized centrifuge is crashed into a jagged crater in the floor like some UFO landing site in a bad B-movie, but still giving off the occasional spark. All across the white tile, glass from downed lights glitter in the flashlight's beam. Then, farther back, the light falls on the open and cloudy eyes of Lincoln's lab mate, Anna. I can't help myself. I rest the light on her bloodied face for a moment, unable to let the beam pass over her like she's only a piece of ruined lab equipment. It's then, the beautiful melody from the phone hiccups. Starting, I take a step back and catch the faintest glimmer in the beam before a computer screen flies through the door. It catches my hip and I go down hard, but roll away from the open door.

Bolero is now interspersed with static and noises that sound like screaming, and I'm up and hobbling for the door to the accelerator as the lights in the antechamber begin to flicker. Reaching out, I punch the code Lincoln gave me into the keypad and watch the light turn from red to green. I open the door and step through, but the door closes behind me. "Fuck!" Spinning around, I open the door and jam the flashlight into the gap to keep it ajar just as something crashes against the other side of the door. Falling back in surprise, I land on the recently injured hip and let out a scream as white-hot pain engulfs my left hip.

Panting now, and fogging up the mask again, I brace against the wall and get to my feet. The lights in this hallway are dim as I grope forward using the wall as my guide. Ahead, the access door to the accelerator is outlined by yellow and black tape. A white sign with red letters on the wall next to it states several safety concerns and precautions, most of which I'm about to or am in the process of violating. I reach the door and find a wheel much like one might find on a submarine hatch. Gripping it with both hands, I begin turning, hoping the physics department follows the rules of "righty-tighty, lefty-loosey." At first, the mechanism is stiff, but with appropriate grunting and swearing, it gives way and turns with increasing speed. I feel the bolt draw back with a clang and pull the door open.

Beyond the door is the accelerator tube. Roughly six-feet in diameter, it sits on struts and stretches on as far as I can see both to my right and left. Passing into the corridor next to the tube, I scan for access panels into the tube itself. One about ten yards down on my right catches my eye as the light on it changes from red to green. Hurrying over to it, I watch as the hatch unseals and begins to open. Warning lights high on the walls come to life and fill the room with red, rotating flashes. At the same time, a klaxon's wail cuts through the mangled instrumental still blaring out of Lincoln's phone.

Before the door opens fully, I'm thrusting my head into the opening, praying the chase is still on while in the back of my mind a terrible thought is taking root. What if it doesn't follow me? What if the WHISP somehow senses Lincoln through the observation room door and waits for him there? It must be able to distinguish between people, and if it knows it can't really hurt me, then why would it follow me?

I just have to pray, with all of the things it could manipulate in the lab, Ray will think there's more machinery and instruments to hurt me within the accelerator. *Does Chester know the accelerator beam can hurt Ray? Does Ray know?*

Inside the tube is like something out of a science fiction movie. The surface is polished copper with multiple lines of bundled wires running into the darkness before me. For being so long, it's a terrifyingly cramped space. Logically, I know the particle beam that will pass through it is thinner than I can fully comprehend, but a more primal part of my brain is urging me to flee before I'm trapped inside and vaporized. Pulling my head back out, I grip the top of the door and use it to help me as I lift my legs up and into the hatch. Next, I push off the door and slide down the side of the tube. It's difficult to remain upright with my suited feet sliding along the curved interior, but I hang on to the hatch opening with my free hand to help keep me upright.

I scan the wall in front of the hatch and spot the video camera I'll use to signal Lincoln. The alarms and warning lights are still flashing, but I bring the phone up to the side of my head and press it to the suit next to my ear. The sweet tones are building and the song is clear. "Fuck." I glance toward the open door in the access hallway. "Come on, you fucker, come and get me."

Seconds tick by and all I can picture is Lincoln on the floor of the observation room beating on the chest of my lifeless husband. Tears drip down my face and blur my already obscured vision. Forgetting it will do no good, I bring the arm holding the phone around to wipe my eyes, and only end up bumping the phone into the mask and dropping it. Out of the corner of my eye, I watch as the phone bounces off the metal wall of the tube and goes sailing off into the dark beyond the reach of the emergency lights. "No! Shit." I release my grip on the hatch opening and immediately drop to my knees as my feet slip out from under me.

Crawling forward in the direction I saw the phone go, I run my gloved hands back and forth and squint down at the bottom of tube. I can't feel anything with the thick gloves and could easily be pushing the phone away from me. Mask fogging over again, I feel blind and deaf inside the suit and without the phone or flashlight I have no way to tell if the WHISP is inside the tube with me. "Fuck it." I sit on my heels as I fumble for the zipper of the radiation suit. I drag the zipper down and rip the mask over my head. When my torso is free of the suit, I find the air is odd and dry and smells like stale plastic, and the walls of the tube are painfully cold to the touch.

I continue on feeling along the tube for the phone with the suit half-on and half-off, dragging it along with my knees. It's easier now because the alarms aren't as loud inside the tube and without the suit I can hear the music again. A few moments later, my fingers close over the cell and I'm scrambling back toward the hatch. *Bolero* is ringing out clear and beautiful and so very surreal. Finding it too hard to crawl with the phone in my hand, I stick it in my mouth and am making good progress until I become conscious of a creaking noise. I glance up and see the light from the hallway growing fainter. At first, I don't know what's happening, but then it makes sense. I let the suit fall away as I stand and lunge forward. The hatch is closing.

I don't know if Lincoln thought I'd given him a sign or if he panicked when I dropped out of sight to pick up the phone, but for whatever reason, he's sealing the accelerator. The phone drops out of my mouth. "No! Not yet! Lincoln, no!" my cries echo around me as the wail of the sirens dampens. I stumble as the curve of the tube's floor throws off my footing and I smack into the wall below the hatch just as the light disappears and the sirens cease. Thrown into blackness, I continue to shout and reach up to try to feel for a manual release. "Lincoln! Open the hatch! It's not in here! Open the hatch!"

All around me, a faint humming thrums through the tube and though I'm no physicist, it gives the distinct impression of a particle accelerator warming up. "Fuck!" I slide back down to the floor of the tube and scrabble around for the radiation suit. The low hum is steadily increasing in pitch when I grab the Tyvek and thrust my feet into legs of the suit. Trying to keep as low as possible, I flip the mask back over my head and claw at the zipper which zips up to just above my waist before snagging on my hospital gown. "Fuck, fuck, fuck!"

As I struggle with the stubborn zipper, the noise from the accelerator is increasing in both pitch and volume. I lay down on my side on the bottom of the tube and use one hand to yank the zipper up while tugging the cheap fabric down with the other. The gown rips, but the zipper still won't budge. "Come on!" In the dark, I can't see what the problem is, and I'm not sure I could fix it even if I could and had the time. Instead, I jam my hands inside the arms of the suit and draw the sides of the suit together as best I can. I then press myself flat against the floor of the tube and wiggle as close to the slope of the wall as I can.

Along the right side of the mask I feel something other than the wall of the tube. Then with another shift Lincoln's phone slips next to my ear. Practically naked, unzipped radiation suit, an assortment of agonies pulsing through me, and knowing the WHISP isn't even in the accelerator with me, a hopeless sob escapes my throat. Squeezing my eyes shut, *Bolero*'s crescendo sounds off in my ear over the rising hum, whirr, and buzz of the accelerator. Even through my closed eyelids, I see the brilliance of a pure, white light. And the world goes silent.

CHAPTER 40

"The FBI arrested Yosev Krimenyonski, the president and CEO of the CryoStep Corporation yesterday in connection with that company's involvement in a criminal WHISP removal service. A spokeswoman for Cryo-Step says the arrest was, quote, 'ridiculous,' citing a lack of clear WHISP therapy centered legislation."

ABC World News

THINGS ARE NICE HERE IN MY QUIET WORLD. I DON'T feel cold, and there's no pain. A pale white light surrounds me as I float on a cushion of cloud for a while, enjoying the numb, nothing sensation until I begin to hear soft music. At first, too soft to make out, soon the notes resolve into a song I recognize, *Bolero*. Then everything turns dark and the cloud gives way beneath me. I'm plummeting faster and faster, sick emptiness rising from my belly into my chest, and then the back of my throat. Lincoln. Ben. Ray. The accelerator. It all comes spiraling back to me.

As my entire body cries out in an aching howl, someone close by groans. *Is there someone in the tunnel with me?* I fight the overwhelming lethargy encasing my body, and after what seems like minutes or hours or months, I crack open an eye. A fuzzy outline of a face looms over me and a band of fear tightens around my heart. But then the face sharpens into Ben's soft features. *Oh God.*

"Did I die?" Upon hearing the ugly scraping sound of my own voice, I know it was my groan I heard before.

Ben chuckles. "You tried, but we wouldn't let you."

I swallow with difficulty.

"I'll get you some water."

His face disappears briefly and behind it the background resolves into a hospital room. My pulse quickens as my mind comes into focus. "Lincoln!" the word is barely a whisper.

Ben reappears, a Styrofoam cup with bendy straw in hand. "Shhh. He's fine. I made him go get some sleep. He's been up for twenty-four hours. He wanted to be here when you woke up." Ben extends the cup toward me, straw aimed at my lips.

A part of me thinks he must be lying. I know Chester's WHISP wasn't in the accelerator with me, so there's no way Lincoln could've gotten away from it. As a cop, I've lied to people before, either to get them to admit to something or to spare them a truth I didn't think they could handle at the time. I sip and let cold water soothe my parched mouth, my sore throat. "What happened?"

"You got it, you got the WHISP."

When my face contorts in confusion, I become aware of bandages covering half of my face and one eye. "How?"

Ben grins. "In the accelerator, just like you said you would."

Terror prickles in my chest as I shake my head minutely. "No, I didn't. The phone...Ray wasn't in there."

Now Ben's brow furrows. "Lincoln saw Ray go in. He said her WHISP was really easy to see in the emergency lights. And when it followed you into the accelerator, he shut the hatch. It must've worked because he's still here."

"But the phone…"

"Lincoln's phone? It exploded. The impact pushed your broken cheekbone out of position. This ringing a bell? You also had a concussion, a bruised ilium, torn hamstring, mild hypothermia…do you want me to go on?"

I try a smile, but it's too painful. "No."

Ben smiles back, but the mirth doesn't quite reach his eyes. There's something he's holding back from me.

"Ben, what is it?"

Squeezing my hand, he takes a deep breath. "Well, several things. Do you want to hear the bad news, the worse news, or the thing I really don't want to tell you?"

The little strength I have is bleeding out of me rapidly. "Let's start with the last one and then we'll go from there."

"It's about Chester." Ben swallows and his eyes shift so he's looking more over my shoulder than into my open eye. "I heard you telling Lincoln about how separating a person from their WHISP can…damage them."

Oh God. I was so caught up in getting us all out alive, I hadn't even considered what destroying Ray would do to Chester. It's one thing to legally sentence a killer like Chester to life behind bars or even death, it's another thing entirely to inflict some unknown mental and psychological damage on them. "What…is she…?"

"She suffered an…episode and is undergoing evaluation."

"Jesus."

Ben's eyes snap back onto mine. "Hey, this isn't your fault. It was self-defense, and now she can't use her WHISP to kill anyone else."

Still reeling, I'm trying to process what I've done, and there's more bad news coming. "What else?"

"Well…there's the small matter of me removing you from this hospital against medical advice the other day and causing a commotion. We're pretty lucky they're so forgiving…and that we have really good insurance; otherwise, we'd both be over at Jersey General right now. I'm pretty sure they still believe in bad spirits, blood-letting, and leeches over there."

I can't smile for him right now, and Ben's weak grin vanishes.

"But seriously, the hospital is charging us a significant fee for them having to engage security. I told them it was a life or death situation, but I'm not sure it's going to matter. I need to call Herb and talk to him about it. I'm hoping, with Herb's magic, we may get off with just a stern warning."

Herb is a wonderful lawyer and a good friend, but I doubt he'll be able to fight with Bellevue. This is more of Ben attempting to distract me. "And the worse news?"

He fidgets and swallows but looks me in the eye. "There's a full-on investigation underway into the death of Lincoln's lab mate, Anna. It… There was a lot of confusion when NYPD and the paramedics showed up at the lab, and Lincoln was trying to get you out of the accelerator and I wasn't in any shape, at the time, to make a statement, and with the way we left the hospital…"

Gears are turning in my head and I'm stepping back from myself, boxing up all of the awful things Ben is telling me and putting them on a shelf. I'm numb again, but not in a pleasant way. This is the clinical anesthesia which keeps a person from having a nervous breakdown. I know because I've felt it before, more than once.

"They think I killed her."

Ben opens his mouth and closes it again, then words tumble out, one falling over the other almost before it's said. "Only some do; obviously, not Crone, but maybe that FBI guy, what's-his-name? But you have to understand, they thought they caught the copycat and then you had that episode at Chester's apartment and then we ran out of the hospital and there are witnesses who saw us driving recklessly and acting strange and

we were at the WHISP protest and you broke into the lab building, and they can't find any other fingerprints and you had her
blood on you from when you thought she was Lincoln and they
don't know Ray was even there..." It's all Ben can get out
before his breath runs out and his voice catches in his throat.

I can see everything up until now has been a mask to
protect me, but now it's cracked and fallen away. He's terrified
I'm going to be convicted of Anna's murder, and somewhere far
away in a container I've chained and padlocked and buried deep
in the ground, I'm also terrified.

CHAPTER 41

"At present, the U.S. military cannot risk the distraction of members with WHISPs. It is not a matter of discrimination, but a matter of risk to human life. Members of the military who develop a WHISP during active duty will be placed into inactive roles."

Statement released by Chairman of the Joint Chiefs of Staff, Brian Hearne

TWENTY-FOUR HOURS LATER, AFTER A MUCH-NEEDED visit from Lincoln and a sponge bath, Crone, Coppola, and the chief stream into my hospital room for the interrogation. My face is still bandaged over my eye, and I'm propped into a sitting position which is uncomfortable for my bruised hipbone, but I try my best to appear serene when they enter. Ben, branded accomplice at worst or biased bystander at best, is forced to wait outside. I want to catch Crone's eye to get an idea of how bad the situation really is, but he's avoiding my gaze, a bad sign. The chief's eyes are like flint and his etched face gives nothing away, and Coppola is showing all the emotion of a dead squirrel. He's the first to speak as he pulls a digital recorder from his pocket, sets it on my bedside table, and turns it on.

"This is the hospital bedside interview of Sylvia Wilma Harbinger, formerly NYPD Lieutenant Harbinger CDS, regarding the death of Anna Kowakowski." Coppola's been addressing the tape recorder, but now he turns his attention on me. "Ms. Harbinger, you've waived your right to have an attorney present at this questioning, is that correct?"

"That's correct."

"Ms. Harbinger, did you kill Anna Kowakowski?"

My mouth hangs open. Trust the FBI to bust straight to the point, but seriously? "No, I did not."

"Did your husband, Benjamin Prieman, or your son Lincoln Prieman kill Anna Kowakowski?"

Now he's just trying to piss me off, but I keep my face neutral and my jaw slack. "No, they did not."

"Do you know who did kill Anna Kowakowski?"

"Yes."

A gleam shines through Coppola's eyes, though I'm not sure what it means. "Who killed her?"

"Technically, Rachel Chester."

His face stiffens. "What do you mean by that?"

Here we go again. I take a deep breath and my cracked ribs protest. "Anna Kowakowski was murdered by Rachel Chester using her WHISP as a weapon."

Coppola ignores this and changes tactics. "Ms. Harbinger, why were you at the lab the day of Anna Kowakowski's murder?"

"I went there to save my son, Lincoln."

"Save your son from what?"

Calm, I must stay calm. They want very badly to dismiss me as a raving madwoman. "From being murdered by Rachel Chester's WHISP."

"Why did you believe your son was in danger?"

"Because Rachel Chester had threatened to murder my son."

His face beginning to tint pink, I'm guessing Coppola expected more rambling incoherency than terse assurance, and I take a very small amount of solace in the knowledge I'm throwing him off balance. In the long run, it won't help my case in the least, but it's a tiny personal victory.

"Why did you believe he was in danger in a secure New York University laboratory building?"

"Because Chester had worked there with him before."

Getting nowhere with me, Coppola switches his approach. "Why were you covered in the victim's blood?"

"Because when I first saw the body, I thought it was my son."

"So?"

"So naturally, I approached the body and in kneeling down beside it, got blood from the blood pool on my legs...probably my hands too."

The gleam is back in Coppola's eyes. "Did you touch the body?"

Shit. I don't want to break eye contact with Coppola, don't want to close my eyes to picture the horror of the moment again and the sick relief which followed when I realized the body wasn't Lincoln's. Staring Coppola down, I'm desperate not to give him an inch, to show no weakness or doubt, but I have to tell the truth. "I don't remember."

"You don't remember?"

"No."

"You might have felt for a pulse or stroked what you thought was your dead son's face, grabbed his hand?"

"It wasn't my son, the body had blonde hair, and when I knelt beside it, I saw that, so I don't think I touched the body, but I can't be certain."

Coppola's expression is cold. "Convenient."

The corners of my mouth flip up mirthlessly. "Not really."

"Did you know Anna Kowakowski had a WHISP?"

"No. I didn't know her, so I couldn't possibly know she had a WHISP."

This breaks Coppola's cool. "You're sure Lincoln didn't tell you about another female student in his lab with a WHISP and you, worried he was working with another psychopath, took matters into your own hands to 'protect' your son?"

It's a pretty good theory considering, and one which gives a hell of a lot more motive than "she just flipped out and randomly started killing people." I have to give Coppola a little credit for it, but it's so wrong it strikes me as funny. "Sorry, no. I didn't even know Lincoln was back working in his old lab until three days ago."

Crone, who has been dead silent up until this point, snorts and Coppola shoots him a scathing look. The chief, for his part, has remained still and impassive as a statue, but the quality of his eyes has maybe softened. Now he steps forward and places a hand on Coppola's shoulder. Coppola has the good grace and survival instinct not to give the chief any dirty looks.

"Please, Ms. Harbinger, tell us what happened in your own words." The chief's voice is a mix of stern concern and professionalism.

He would never let our history together bias his judgement, and I haven't yet given him any proof of my innocence, so I can't blame him for not being on my side. Still, I can't say the lack of support doesn't hurt.

"Of course. Where would you like me to begin?"

"Why don't you start with your disruptive outburst here at this hospital and your flight from hospital security?"

"All right." I clear my throat and prepare to unload the whole story as dry as I can possibly make it, but then there's a knock at the door.

"What is it?" Coppola takes three long strides to the door and wretches it open.

I can't see who's on the other side, but I can hear them.

"Sir, I'm sorry. There's a call from forensics, Sir. They've been trying to reach you. They say it's extremely urgent."

Coppola's face turns a darker shade of red. Spinning on his heel, he returns to the side of my bed and picks up the recorder. "We're not finished here. I'll be back in a few minutes." He gives me a dark look, then raises his gaze to the chief and waves him toward the door. "Chief."

The chief nods and walks to the door without even giving me a sideways glance. Coppola follows him, and Crone is the last to leave. Just before exiting, he turns and gives me a thumbs up, and I feel a prickle of tears in my eye.

CHAPTER 42

"...I am the shadow the shadows must fear. I am the light in the darkness who will dispel the phantoms who walk among us. WHISPs are the enemy. Humanity will know my name..."

Excerpt from an anonymous letter posted to the Chicago Tribune

THEY DON'T LET BEN OR ANYONE ELSE VISIT IN THE interim, and as the minutes stretch out to an hour, I start to doze. I'm shocked when I open my eyes and just Crone is there.

"Am I dreaming or is this all part of some sadistic bad cop, good cop routine where you're the good cop?"

A wide smile drapes itself across his mouth. "Heh, good one. No, you'd know better than to trust me, I hope. I just came to give you the good news."

"What good news?"

"Well, I'm not sure if you knew this, but the lab was equipped with a bunch of really fancy cameras."

I shrug. "So what? Cameras don't work with WHISPs around."

His eyes sparkle. "Ahh, normal cameras don't work with

WHISPs around, but these are special cameras designed to withstand the...um...designed to work around a lot of weird shit, like what goes on in a physics lab."

"Okay." My mind is churning with new possibilities. Maybe the camera in the access hallway actually picked up Ray. It wouldn't mean I'd be completely off the hook, but what I did would look a lot less crazy if there's video of a WHISP chasing me and throwing a computer at me.

"And..." Crone's furtive glance takes in the room as if he's expecting someone to leap out from under the bed or from behind the nightstand. He edges closer and pulls out his cell phone. "There's something on the tape I thought you might want to see." His chubby fingers work over the screen and then he angles the phone so we can both watch the video playing on it.

Initially, it's a blank, black and white, wide angle looking down on roughly half the lab outside the accelerator areas. After a few seconds, a girl with long blonde hair pulled back into a neat ponytail, presumably Anna, ambles into frame carrying a clipboard onto which she is making notes. Then the lights flicker and the girl's head tilts up so she's staring at the lights. A few more seconds pass with her staring upwards and then right when she seems to have come to a decision about them, her own WHISP, barely visible except in certain flickers of the light, moves.

But it doesn't just move, the head part looks down and over the girl's shoulder out in front of her and then the whole body of if turns away from the girl and appears as if it's trying to get away. Moments later, the recording begins to blur and show static, but still visible is the grotesque scene unfolding in the camera's field. The girl freezes, her whole body tensing until the lines of taut muscles stand out against her skin while all the while her WHISP is still squirming and lurching away. Then I can see a faint outline of shadow as its hands wind around the girl's throat. Knowing what's going to happen next, I turn my head and shield my face with my hand.

"Turn it off."

"I thought you'd want to see how it works, finally." There's a slight injured quality to Crone's voice.

"Not anymore."

He pockets the phone. "Well, that's it, then. Proof."

I want to believe it. "They'll question it. There's some distortion."

"There's also a time stamp, and the time stamp says you and your hubby were driving like maniacs through a red light when this happened. Both of you are even visible in the shot."

Now I let loose the smile I've been keeping tethered. "I could kiss you right now, Crone."

Rolling his eyes, he chuckles. "Try to refrain yourself, Harbinger. I didn't do anything but tell tech to double check those cameras."

My smile slips. "Tell me about Chester."

Crone frowns me down. "Don't do this to yourself. She was trying to kill your whole fucking family."

"Crone."

He sighs and throws his hands in the air. "She had some kind of seizure. Fortunately, they made her wear a biosensor since her freak out with you and they got to her pretty quick. She's conscious, but yeah, there was some damage and she's not exactly right, well less so than she was. The docs aren't sure if it's temporary or permanent."

"Is...she in pain?"

"No...well, I don't think so."

"Well, I guess that's something."

Shaking his head, Crone points a finger at me. "Seriously, forget about Rachel Chester. She's already fucked your life up enough." He drops his arm. "I'd say I'm sorry I ever let the chief bring you in on this case, but seeing as how you solved the damn thing, guess I can't."

"Oh, you let the chief bring me in. I'm sure he'd be interested to hear that." I'm trying to be cheerful, given my having just narrowly beaten a murder rap, but there's one more thing bothering me. "They're going to overturn her conviction, aren't they?"

"Probably. Given this clear evidence the WHISP did it."

"But she was there at the first murders. We know that."

Crone's eyebrows shoot up.

"I know, I know, it doesn't mean she made the WHISP do it or could've stopped it. The best we can get her on now is what, breaking and entering? Fuck."

"You've got to let it go. With the WHISP gone, there's no way to prove she was controlling it, absolutely none."

I nod, not sure I'll be able to. "Dammit, all this is going to do is create more WHISP hate."

"Hey, WHISPs don't kill people, psychopaths with WHISPs kill people." Crone's face is sober.

The silence between us lasts maybe all of five seconds before we both burst into wonderful, irreverent, side-pinching guffaws. I let the cathartic laughter bubble out of me until tears are running down my cheeks.

"Thanks, I needed that."

"Hey, what are partners for?" He wipes his eyes. "Now, you get some more rest, because I know you've got like a four-day drive coming up pretty soon here. I hear Montana is beautiful this time of year."

"Yeah, it is…"

"Now you better go enjoy your fucking early retirement." Crone turns and ambles over to the door.

As he opens it, I rack my brain for the perfect thing to say. "Hey, Crone."

He turns. "Yeah, Harbinger."

"What's your first name?"

He turns away, takes a deep breath, lets it out. "Dwight."

"Thanks, Dwight."

He raises a hand, but doesn't look back. The door swings shut behind him.

CHAPTER 43

"WHISPs are nothing if not reflections of a society evolving, but it is not evolution as it is in nature. It is not survival of the fittest, but rather a manmade evolution of survival of the more technologically advanced. But beware. Technology is not always advancement, and when we rely on it too much, we lose our own precious ability to adapt to a changing world."

Archer Cam, Environmental Priest

"WELL, THAT'S THE LAST ONE." BEN PUTS THE TAPE dispenser aside and rises gingerly, placing the box on top of a stack of similar cardboard boxes all neatly labeled in black Sharpie.

Padding over, I kiss him and run my fingers through his filling beard. "You know, you're pretty spry for a man who had a spike of metal speared through his leg less than two weeks ago."

"Oh yeah? Well, you're pretty cute for...well, you're just pretty cute."

I kiss him again. "Why thank you, Mr. Bearded Mountain Man."

"I thought it was appropriate, considering we're moving to the wilds of Montana. You seem to like it."

"I do." I slide my hands down from his face and around his waist and pull him into a hug.

"Whoa, what's this for?"

"Have I told you lately how much I appreciate you not bleeding out and dying?"

Ben releases me and takes a step back. "Only about as often as I tell you how much I appreciate you risking your life in a goddamn particle accelerator to save my life...and Lincoln's."

"Pah, it was easy. All I had to do was climb inside a big tube. You had to keep your blood inside your veins."

"Funny..." Furrows form between Ben's fuzzy brows. "Wait a minute, too funny. Sylvy, what's going on?"

My smile is more of a straight line. "Maybe nothing. Come sit down, I made us some coffee..." I head for our bare kitchen and card table with two chairs we've been using as a kitchen table. "And by made coffee, I mean, snuck out to Java's Cup 'O' Joe and got you a large hazelnut latte with a splash of caramel."

Ben limps in behind me and winces. "Oh crap. I'm not going to like this, am I?"

I sit, pat the seat next to me, and push the coffee toward him. Then I open the white box on the table. "I also got us crullers from Haversham's Bakery."

Ben slumps down into the chair and frowns. "Now you've got me really scared." He snatches a cruller from the box and jams half of it in his mouth. After making a show of rolling his eyes back in his head and chewing blissfully for several seconds, he swallows and uses the other half of the cruller to jab at me. "Stop buttering me up and get to." He then shoves the rest of the cruller in his mouth and takes the lid off his coffee, inhaling deeply.

"Okay, so I know that we just finished packing up everything we own and are getting ready to move across seven states, but what if we didn't do that?"

The chewing ceases and Ben just stares at me. I avoid his gaze and instead sip at my coffee. Eventually, he finishes off the cruller, takes a sip of his own coffee and clears his throat.

"Instead we would what? Keeping in mind, of course, neither of us has a job now and we've given notice on the apartment and have"—he checks his watch—"oh, about five minutes in which to vacate the premises."

"Well, there's a new task force being put together."

"Task force?"

"To, ah, handle WHISP-related crimes."

Ben's mouth falls open. "WHISP-related crimes?"

"Yes. Apparently, since the circumstances of Chester's case went public, there's been an increased awareness of the potential for people to use their WHISPs for illegal purposes and an increase in WHISP hate crimes, and the NYPD wants to make sure both are handled properly."

"Okaay. Still not seeing the connection between this task force thingy and us."

"Well, they're looking for people with direct...um...experiences with WHISPs."

His eyebrows skyrocket. "And by"—Ben uses his fingers to make air quotes—"'experiences,' do you mean, almost killed by?"

"Um, yeah, something like that."

Ben buries his face in his hands. "You cannot be serious, Sylvy. After all we've been through. After all that *you've* been through. Sweetie, why on God's green earth would we subject ourselves to something like that again? I thought you wanted to get away from all this WHISP stuff. I thought you wanted to retire."

I touch the side of his face. "I did. But things change. Do

you know I haven't had a nightmare about my folks since Ray tried to kill us? It's like all my fears were much worse than the actual thing. Dr. Fritz says it's something to do with subconscious realization of...um...reality? Also, it's not like I can really hide anymore." I jab a thumb behind me at the wisp of a WHISP mimicking my every movement. Turns out being inside a particle accelerator with an unzipped radiation suit is a good way to earn a WHISP of your very own. "Anyways, it wouldn't be full time, and we'd have a whole team working with us."

"Wait, wait, wait, hold on, we, us, what the hell would they want with me? I'm not a cop."

"No, but you're a physicist. There's a whole new field of WHISP particle physics and the task force has funding from the federal government for research. You'd have your own lab."

Ben sticks out his lower lip. "Maybe I don't want my own lab."

"Lincoln wants you to have your own lab. He wants to work in your lab...in fact...they may have already recruited him and he may have already said yes."

"What! What the hell, Sylvy? How could you not tell me that?"

"Lincoln and I wanted to keep it a secret until I got a chance to think things over."

Amused annoyance has transformed into anger and Ben's face goes crimson. "This is bullshit. This is blackmail or intimidation or some shit."

"You're right, I'm sorry. I just...I honestly didn't know what I wanted to do, and I didn't want the same thing to happen to me with you and Lincoln ganging up."

Ben stands and walks over to the sink. Turning, he folds his arms. "I would've never done that to you."

"I know. And I'm not even sure I want to do this. I wouldn't have waited until the night before we left if I was sure. But I feel like once we leave, there's no coming back, like if I decide in a month or a week or even tomorrow, I want to take this opportunity, it'll be too late."

Staring at the floor and working his jaw, Ben is silent.

"I think I need to do this, Ben. I think I've finally faced my fears, but there's more to it, like I also need to make amends for...I don't know, for having these fears in the first place? No, that doesn't make sense. For..." Words flutter around in my head like butterflies. "Ugh, it's just, I've done so much damage with Chester... Do you understand?"

The only sound in the kitchen is of Ben breathing deeply in and out through his nose. I'm afraid to move. I don't know which decision is the right one, but my gut is telling me to stay. Even if we didn't join the taskforce, we would still be close to Lincoln, and I wouldn't feel like I'm running away with my tail between my legs. I wouldn't feel like Chester beat me after all. But then again, there's always the benefits of a clean break, a fresh start. I might've been right before when I thought leaving the city behind could be exactly what Ben and I need to put everything behind us and move forward, unhindered by the past.

Ben stirs. "Okay. But where the hell are we going to live?"

Leaping out of the chair, I throw my arms around his neck. "We'll figure something out."

"Sylvy, are you *sure* you want to do this?"

Kissing him, everything that has felt wrong and out of place over the last week falls neatly in line. "I am now."

SNEAK PEEK AT WHISPERS OF TERROR

WHISPS BOOK TWO

When the newly formed WHISP task force is called in to investigate a kidnapping and possible bioterrorism attack, NYPD Detective Sylvia Harbinger finds herself the middle-woman between the NYPD and an extremist anti-WHISP organization, exposed to a WHISP virus, and having lengthy conversations with her own recently formed WHISP. Or is she only talking to herself?

With Ben and Lincoln backing her in the task force laboratory, she races to find the kidnapping victims and a cure, yet the terrorists always seem to keep one step ahead. Sylvia's running out of leads and out of time, but giving up isn't an option. One of the lives she saves may be her own.

CHAPTER 1

In every murmur, a breath of fear

KIRBY IS AN UGLY BUILDING. EVEN WITH THE SUN'S morning rays lighting its impressively tall face, there is nothing pretty about it: no fancy trim to the stone, no statuary, and no pillars. The fact that it houses and treats New York City's criminally insane doesn't help, and the fact that I'm here to visit Rachel Chester really doesn't help. I promised Dr. Fritz I'd see her as part of my therapy, but right now, I'm frozen outside the front doors choking on a bone-dry throat.

It's a totally different sensation from seeing her in Rikers, a totally different fear. This isn't the diabolical murderer trying to invade my head and unravel my psyche. This is the woman I literally drove insane by destroying her WHISP. And I did it knowing what would happen to her. Never mind that her WHISP was trying to murder me and my family at the time, and that she was probably controlling it...probably.

I catch my reflection in the glass, but I can't see my own WHISP today. Not in this bright sunlight. If I just stay in the sun I can pretend none of this ever happened. I can imagine

Chester's still in Rikers atoning for her crimes; I can believe I never jumped in a particle accelerator and developed a WHISP.

Honestly, I could come back another day. But that's a lie. I know if I don't go in now, I will never enter this building again...at least, not willingly.

Every step is like walking through molasses, but I make it to the doors then through them to the security checkpoint. The guard makes me leave my gun. It was stupid to bring it, but it's habit, and if I'm honest, a bit of a security blanket. At reception, a woman with a lovely floral hijab smiles across the counter at me.

"Hello. How can I help you today?"

Deep breath. I take out my badge, also habit. "Hello. My name's Detective Harbinger. I'm here to see Rachel Chester."

The smile evaporates. "I'm sorry, Detective, but Ms. Chester has a very limited number of approved visitors—"

"I'm on the list."

She consults her computer screen. "I see"—then points to a sign-in sheet. "Sign there. I'll call for a security officer to take you."

I hadn't really considered Chester would be in a secure area, but why wouldn't she be? She was a murderer, or her WHISP had been, and who could say what she was capable of without Ray?

"Detective?"

From seemingly out of nowhere, the guard has appeared. Young, but with the dour expression of an eighty-year-old widower, he points to the elevators beyond reception. The chill of the receptionist follows me as we walk away, and I'm not sure if she's put off by my WHISP or if she knows I'm the one who put Chester in here. My escort, name badge Raymond, of all names, says nothing as we enter the elevator. He pushes the 10.

There's no music, so the silence stretches like a piano

string, broken only by the ping of the change of floors. I'd love to break the tension, but the walls are closing in and I can't think of a single thing to say other than, "Oh god, oh god, oh god." When the doors finally open, I nearly burst out ahead of Raymond, but manage to stay a step behind him as we head down a white hallway lined with white doors. After we pass an unmanned attendant's station, he stops abruptly and turns.

"Ms. Chester has been in a catatonic state for three months, but don't try to touch her, give her anything, take anything from her, or touch any of her monitors or her IV's. If you think there's a medical problem, there's a red button on the wall near the door to summon a nurse. Otherwise, I will return in fifteen minutes to take you back out. All visits are restricted to fifteen minutes for non-family members. Do you have any questions?"

Locked in a room with Rachel Chester for fifteen minutes. *Is she strapped down? Can I have my gun back?* I shake my head.

He continues down the hall, stops in front of room 1026, and pulls out a card dangling from a lanyard around his neck. My gut tightens as I scan the hallway. It's completely empty. No, that's probably not true. I'm sure there are other manned stations, just recessed so I can't see them. Holding my breath, I hope to catch the chit-chat of nurses between medication distributions but there's only a muffled scream.

"I'll be back in fifteen minutes." Raymond opens a small window at the top of the door and looks through it before swiping his card across a pad next to the door and pulling it open.

Every fiber in my body is telling me to run, to bolt back to the elevator. You don't want to see this! Inside, is a cheerful, if Spartan, room with yellow walls and a hospital bed. Chester sits in a wheelchair facing the single window streaming in sunlight. Next to her an IV stand and portable monitor unit whir softly. The scent of disinfectant hangs in the air, under it sweat, old saliva, and human waste.

You can do this. I will myself into the room and the door shuts behind me. Terror grips me. *What if Ray is hiding in the sunlight?* But, of course, she…it…isn't. I saw to that. *Could she…it…grow back?* I could just stand here the whole fifteen minutes, then answer honestly when Dr. Fritz asked if I'd visited Chester. *Yes, I visited her. I was in her room for fifteen minutes.* But I've come all this way. I have to look her in the eye. Not for him, for me.

Hugging the wall, I edge closer to the figure in the wheel-chair. I should probably say something, but I can't break the silence, can't stop listening to the whirr of the machines and the soft whisper of Chester's breathing. I can almost see her face now, but a greasy curtain of her hair is in the way. Strands of it billow with every breath. My own breaths are jagged, my heart clogging my throat. Just a few more steps.

Everything goes white as Chester's face comes into view. I'm blinded by the sunlight, my roaring blood blocks out every sound, but eventually I adjust. Here is the monster of my dreams. She looks sad. Drooping, sallow skin houses a shell of a person. Blank eyes stare into the light, seeing nothing. My heart slows, but each beat is painful. She wasn't a good person, but she doesn't deserve this. *What have I done?*

I'm sorry.

I can't say the words aloud. *But she could recover, couldn't she?* A few years of healing, of therapy, and she could be a person again. We don't know this is permanent. Any moment, she could jump out of that chair and try to strangle me, just like old times. I know I'm reaching, but it's all I have. I open my mouth: *Snap out of it!* But I can't form the words.

A bit of foam has gathered at the corner of her open mouth, and as I stare, one of the bubbles pops. Thoughts break free of my subconscious prison and ruthlessly hurl to the surface of my brain.

That could be you.

CHAPTER 2

Fritz: What about your physical relationship with Ben since the change?
Harbinger: That's actually going surprisingly well.
Fritz: Does that bother you?
Harbinger: Why would it bother me?
Fritz: You tell me.

Excerpt from Transcript of Session 47:
Dr. Aziz Fritz with Det. S. Harbinger

"ADMIT IT, IT'S WEIRD."

Ben blinks, his eyes straying over my shoulder into the shadows beyond then back again. "What? No."

"You're cute when you're lying." I boop his nose with my finger. Ben, my Ben. We're tangled up in sheets, basking in the euphoria of a renewed partnership, a revitalized marriage fueled by a shared near-death experience and reunion of our small family. A year ago, I couldn't have imagined being on a special WHISP task force with both my husband and my son. In fact, Ben and I were supposed to have been in a tech-free cabin in Montana by now, sheltered from all things WHISP. That ship sailed when I climbed into a particle accelerator and got one of my own.

To say I'm still adjusting is an understatement. After a year, I swear there's a pull in the center of my back from the invisible tether between us. I still flinch sometimes when I catch a glimpse of it, and get the sense of someone following me all the time, though the smothering panic attacks are very rare now. Most of the time, I just try to forget it's there. My therapist is constantly reminding me how unhealthy this attitude is, but I've gotten pretty good at ignoring him, too.

Ben sighs. "Okay, okay. Sometimes it's weird, but only…"

"When I'm on top?"

"When I can see her."

My eyebrows twitch. *"Her?"*

"It. I meant, it."

His backpedaling obvious, I raise onto an elbow and stare him down. "Please don't tell me you've named my WHISP. That's worse than naming my boobs."

He smirks and reaches out for a gentle grope. "I thought you liked their nicknames."

I bat his hand away and sit up. "Don't change the subject. Did you name it?" I want to be amused that my particle scientist husband studying the WHISP phenomenon at its basic level would name mine. It would be akin to an oncologist naming a tumor. But after dealing with Rachel Chester's murderous WHISP, "Ray," I can't find the humor I'm searching for. Irritation itches at the insides of my throat, spoiling the post-coital glow.

"It's not…" He sits up and starts again. "I didn't want to, but one day it just popped into my head and I couldn't get it out."

"Couldn't get what out?"

Ben's skin has paled and taken on a green sheen. His eyes flit away from mine then back again.

"Ben—"

"Liv."

"Liv?" As images of a rock star's actress daughter force their way into my head, the tingles of a smile pull at the corners of my mouth, but they're smothered when I realize it's just a bastardization of my name, like Rachel to Ray.

Ben must see the disgust in my face. "I'm sorry, babe, I know it's..."

"Fucked up?"

"Similar."

I close my eyes and let myself fall back onto my pillow. How long is Rachel fucking Chester going to ruin my life? But really, would any name be better? Jo, Marie, Consuela, Anastasia, Nefertiti...Bob? Liv. I have to admit, the name seems to fit. Am I just pissed because I didn't get to name her myself? No, not her, *it*. Oh, who am I kidding? Liv is totally a chick. My little chicky WHISP. I imagine her under the bed now staring up at the underside of the box springs. When a chill runs through me, I open my eyes.

Ben is staring. "I'm sorry."

I reach up and rub his beard scruff. "I know. It's okay. I mean, it's not okay, okay, but it's okay. It could be worse. Liv is kinda sexy." I'm really trying here.

"Yeah?" Ben kisses the mound between my thumb and forefinger.

Not going to happen now. The sound of Lincoln's shower turning on saves me having to disappoint Ben on the possibility of a round two. My mind flickers to memories of round one and I wonder again about the thickness of Lincoln's apartment walls and cringe inwardly.

"He probably won't hear us in the shower." Ben raises an eyebrow in mock hope.

My other excuse; I point to the clock as a reminder of an earlier, hastily pressed snooze button.

He groans, falling back onto the bed. "Just five more minutes."

I lean over him and kiss him on the nose. "Five minutes more was ten minutes ago."

He opens his eyes and frowns. "I really am sorry. I love you, and I don't want you to think...anything's changed."

"Everything's changed, but I know what you mean."

My cell buzzes on the nightstand and I glance at the clock again. Seven fifty. Almost eight. Almost an appropriate time for someone to call, but not quite. My cop sense comes to life and washes over me like a splash of cold water. I reach for the phone with cold fingers. It's the station. "Harbinger."

"I'd good morning you, Detective, but I don't want to blow smoke up your ass, because we both know that's not true."

Crone isn't officially on the task force, but many of our cases have started as his. "What happened?"

"Hate crime, looks like. Someone hit a WHISP shelter last night."

"Shit. How many?"

"One, for sure."

"Only one?" A single WHISP murder, even at a shelter, wouldn't justify an early morning phone call.

"For sure. There's an unknown number missing from the shelter."

"Missing. Okay." Still not worth this phone call. "What else?"

Crone clears his throat. "There's a guy here from CAW who wants to talk to you about it."

There it is. "An informant?"

"More like a spokesperson. He wants to clear their name in this."

"Kinda early for that, isn't it? If this just happened last night, how did they even know about it already? Seems a little 'the lady doth protest too much,' doesn't it?"

If Crone gets the reference, he doesn't let on. "Are you coming in, or what?"

"Be there in thirty." I let out a long sigh. Not as bad a call as it could've been this early in the morning.

Ben wraps his arms around me from the side, I note, not behind. "New case?"

I nod. "New case."

———

ON THE WAY TO THE STATION, I ANSWER MY OWN question. Of course, CAW would know about the shelter. They're probably watching all things WHISP closer than even our little task force is. Still, something smells funny. True, CAW, Citizens Against WHISPs, would be the first people we'd want to talk to about a crime like this, yet them heading us off at the pass is strange. I have visions of CAW's preeminent lawyer, Lila Grant, in her tastefully revealing suit in the interrogation room, but when I arrive at the station, I can already tell by Crone's sullen demeanor that he hasn't seen anything he liked this morning.

"What took you so long? Up late at a kegger last night?" Crone chuckles at his own joke.

He's been giving me shit about me and Ben temporarily living with Lincoln, still technically a college student working on his Master's thesis, while we search for a new apartment. I ignore him and point toward interrogation. "So?"

Crone thumbs over his shoulder toward the conference room. "Apparently, we aren't treating Mr. McCaffrey as a suspect quite yet."

"Mr. McCaffrey?"

Crone opens a file. "Rondell James McCaffrey, thirty-three, previously arrested for petty theft at age fifteen for shoplifting, used to work at a Kwik Lube, now currently employed full-time by CAW as a public relations specialist."

"How does a grease monkey become a public relations specialist?"

"Good question."

I raise my eyebrows at him. "You didn't ask him anything?"

Crone shrugs. "He says he'll only talk to you. Probably wants your autograph for taking out Ray."

My gut tightens. Yeah, Rachel Chester's WHISP was trying to kill me and my family, but destroying it broke something in Chester. Having her behind bars because of me was justice, but having her in a psyche ward because of me is something else. "Nah, no one at CAW would want my autograph now that I've got a WHISP." I grab the file from Crone. "Anything you wanna tell me about the crime before I go in there? There's a body, right?"

Crone's grubby fingers snatch up another file on his desk. "Yosef Zimmerman, fifty-eight. There's a Brooklyn address on his driver's license we're following up, but it seemed like he was in residence at the WHISP shelter, so he probably had a WHISP. Nothing weird with his murder though, he was just shot."

"Could he have been the target and the other residents just scattered?"

Crone shrugs again. "We're searching for surveillance footage from traffic cams and nearby buildings. We'll probably know more in a few hours." He grins. "You could just get this guy to confess CAW did it and save us all a lot of time."

"Wouldn't that be nice?" I head toward the conference room.

"Go get 'em, tiger."

Behind my back, I give Crone the finger. I wonder if he can see my WHISP doing the same.

www.scarsdalepublishing.com

CPSIA information can be obtained
at www.ICGtesting.com
Printed in the USA
LVHW111504180920
666491LV00001B/86